PRAISE FOR
THE WILD ROBOT

'A powerful and enchanting meditation on the nature of wildness itself . . . Will pull at any heartstrings, human or mechanical'
Piers Torday, author of *The Last Wild*

'*The Wild Robot* has all the pathos and grace of *The Iron Giant* or a Studio Ghibli animation. It is nonetheless its own thing, a delicate, touching tale of survival, friendship and family' *Financial Times*

'A modern-day classic in the making' Booktrust

'A heartfelt story . . . about how even the oddest of us can find friends – we need Peter Brown to tell his fellow Americans how what seems strange and threatening can turn into love and joy'
New Statesman

'Robot sentience meets maternal love in the renowned author-illustrator Peter Brown's first foray into writing for older children, *The Wild Robot*. It has a simplicity and directness that masks unfathomable depths' *Times Literary Supplement*

'Brown has written a lively tale that is sure to engage young readers'
The New York Times

'Roz may not feel emotions, but young readers certainly will as this tender, captivating tale unfolds' *Washington Post*

'An uplifting story about an unexpected visitor whose arrival disrupts the animal inhabitants of a rocky island, with a contemporary twist . . . Brown wisely eschews a happy ending in favour of an open-ended one that supports the tone of a story that's simultaneously unsentimental and saturated with feeling'
Publishers Weekly, starred review

Also by Peter Brown

THE WILD ROBOT

THE WILD ROBOT ESCAPES

THE WILD ROBOT ESCAPES

WORDS AND PICTURES BY
PETER BROWN

Piccadilly
PRESS

First published in 2018 by Little, Brown and Company,
a division of Hachette Book Group, 1290 Avenue of the Americas,
New York, NY 10104, USA

First published in Great Britain in 2018 by
PICCADILLY PRESS
80–81 Wimpole St, London W1G 9RE
www.piccadillypress.co.uk

A CIP catalogue record for this book is available from the British Library.

ISBN: 978-1-84812-751-7
also available as an ebook

1

Printed and bound in Great Britain by Clays Ltd, Elcograf S.p.A.

Piccadilly Press is an imprint of Bonnier Zaffre Ltd,
a Bonnier Publishing company
www.bonnierpublishing.com

To the wild places of the future

CHAPTER I

THE CITY

Our story begins in a city, with buildings and streets and bridges and parks. Humans were strolling, automobiles were driving, airships were flying, robots were hard at work.

Weaving through the city streets was a delivery truck. The truck knew where to go, and how to get there, all by itself. It pulled up to a construction site and automatically unloaded some crates. A few more turns and it unloaded more crates down at the docks. The truck

zigged

and

zagged

across the city, delivering crates as it went, and then it merged onto a highway.

Cars and buses and trucks were cruising along the highway together. But as the delivery truck continued, the traffic became lighter, the buildings became smaller, and the landscape became greener.

With nothing but open road ahead, the truck accelerated to its top speed. The landscape outside was now just a green blur, occasionally broken by a flicker of gray as a town flew past. On and on the delivery truck went, racing over long bridges, shooting through mountain tunnels, gliding down straight stretches of highway, until it started to slow. It drifted from the fast lane to the exit lane, and then it rolled down a ramp and into farm country.

Clouds of dust billowed up behind the truck as it drove past fields and fences. In the hazy distance, enormous barns loomed above the plains. The air was thick with the smells of soil and livestock. Robot crews methodically worked the crops and fed the animals and operated the massive farm machines.

A hill gradually climbed into view. The hill was crowned with trees and white buildings. Another farm. But this one was smaller and shabbier than the rest. Out front was a crooked sign that read *Hilltop Farm*.

Wheels crunched on gravel as the delivery truck rolled onto the driveway and up to the top of the hill. It stopped beside the front porch of the farmhouse and dropped its last crate to the ground. Then the truck drove away.

Reader, can you guess what was tightly packed inside that crate? If you guessed a robot, you're correct. But this was no ordinary robot. It was ROZZUM unit 7134. You might remember her old life on a remote, wild island. Well, Roz's new life was just about to begin.

THE CRATE

Woof! Woof! Woof!

Inside the farmhouse, a dog was barking and scraping at the front door. When the door finally opened, the dog scurried out and bounced down the porch steps. And then a man appeared.

The man walked with a limp, and slowly made his way down to the crate, where his dog was sniffing around. He unlatched the top of the crate and it swung open on its hinges. Packing foam was tossed aside, restraining cords were unfastened, and there was ROZZUM unit 7134. Her lifeless body sparkled in the late-day sun.

The man reached down and pressed an important little button on the back of the robot's head.

Click.

CHAPTER 3
THE ROBOT

The robot's computer brain booted up and her programs began coming online. Then she automatically stood, stepped out of her crate, and started to speak.

"Hello, I am ROZZUM unit 7134, but you may call me Roz. While my robotic systems are activating, I will tell you about myself.

"Once fully activated, I will be able to move and communicate and learn. Simply give me a task and I will complete it. Over time, I will find better ways of completing my tasks. I will become a better robot. When I am not needed, I will stay out of the way and keep myself in good working order.

"Thank you for your time.

"I am now fully activated."

CHAPTER 4

THE FAMILY

"*Welcome to Hilltop Farm*, Roz. My name is Mr. Shareef. You belong to me now."

Roz studied the man with her softly glowing eyes and in a robotic voice she said, "Hello, Mr. Shareef."

"This old fella here is Oscar." Mr. Shareef scratched his dog's head. "You won't see much of him. Oscar spends most of his time sleeping in the house."

"Hello, Oscar," said the robot.

A goofy grin stretched across the dog's face and he let out a happy yelp.

Mr. Shareef pulled a small computer from his pocket. He tapped the screen and brought up a map of Hilltop Farm. "There you are, Roz," he said as the robot's electronic signal appeared on the map. "You'll be working all over this farm. And now that you're in the system I can always see right where you are."

"What would you like me to do?" said Roz.

"You can start by putting your crate in the garage over there. I'll hold on to it, in case I ever have to send you back to the factory."

Clearly, Roz was designed to take orders, because her body automatically did as it was told. She stuffed the packing materials into her crate and carried it into the garage.

When Roz returned, Mr. Shareef was watching a school bus winding along the country road. Oscar barked and dashed off as the bus came to a stop at the bottom of the driveway. A girl and a boy jumped out, and the bus drove on. In their matching school uniforms, the children looked almost identical. But the boy was a little taller, and the girl's hair was a little longer. They meandered up the driveway and romped around with their dog until they noticed Roz.

"A robot!" said the girl, running up.

"It's about time we got one," said the boy.

"She's refurbished," said the man. "She's the cheapest one I could find, but she'll make a decent farmer."

"What's her name?" said the girl.

"She said her name's Roz."

"That's just her starter name," said the boy. "We can give her any name we want. Let's call her...Farmbot!"

"I kind of like the name Roz," said the girl.

"Me too," said Mr. Shareef. "Let's leave her name as it is. Roz, I'd like you to meet my daughter, Jaya, and my son, Jad."

"Hello, Jaya and Jad," said the robot.

The children looked at each other and smiled.

"Will Roz take orders from me?" asked Jad.

"What about me?" asked Jaya.

"She'll take orders from both of you."

"Roz, I order you to do my homework!" said Jaya.

"Don't waste her time with nonsense!" Mr. Shareef grumbled. "Roz is here to do farmwork, not homework, understand?"

The children nodded.

"Now, I order you kids to bring the dog inside and do your own homework," said Mr. Shareef. "I need to show Roz the farm."

CHAPTER 5

THE FARM

Mr. Shareef turned and shouted, "Come here, Rambler!"
A moment later, a pickup truck automatically rolled out
from the garage. The truck pulled up to the man and the
robot, its doors opened wide, and they both climbed in.

Rambler had a steering wheel,
but Mr. Shareef sat back and let
the truck drive itself. They
followed the driveway
behind the house, across
the backyard, past
trees and hedges,
and suddenly they

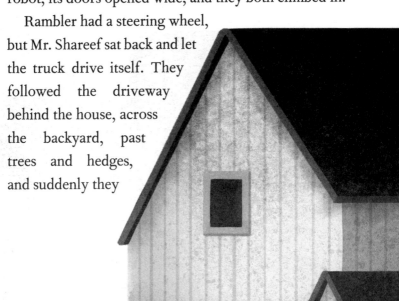

were surrounded by farm buildings. The buildings were different sizes and shapes, all white walls with gray roofs, and they were so tightly packed together that you could hardly tell where one building ended and the next one began. Some were spattered with mud. Others had holes and loose boards. The entire place smelled like grass and manure.

Mr. Shareef pointed out each building to Roz. There was the enormous dairy barn, the milking parlor, the workshop, the machine shed. Smaller sheds were scattered all around.

Rambler drove out from the buildings and down the back side of the hill into a wide sweep of farmland. A fence lined this part of the driveway, and behind the fence was a sprawling, rolling pasture, lush with tall grass and a few leafy trees, where a herd of cows was grazing. The cows swished their tails and chewed their cud and followed the truck with their eyes. One of them let out a long "Moooooo."

"This is a dairy farm," said Mr. Shareef, "so these cows are the queens around here. Your whole world now revolves around them. Understand?"

"I understand," said Roz as she stared at a young calf who was staring right back at her.

They rolled past the herd of cows, past clumps of wildflowers, past a quiet pond, past birds and field mice and bumblebees. The driveway cut through a row of trees on its way out to the crop fields, which were flat and square and covered with bright green sprouts.

Hilltop Farm was bursting with life, but it had seen better days. Patches of weeds and bare dirt were spreading across the fields. Broken-down farm machines and piles of junk were strewn across the grounds. Thick tangles of brush were creeping in from the edges of the property.

They drove all the way out to the farthest fields, to a little roundabout at the very end of the driveway. Rambler shut off its engine, and the man and the robot sat and looked at the countryside.

Far off, where the land met the sky, a train quietly slid along its tracks and disappeared to the north. Then all was still.

"This farm needs help," said Mr. Shareef at last. "It's been in my family for generations and I don't want to lose it. But I can't do farmwork anymore, not with this bad leg. That's why you're here. They say ROZZUM robots can learn to do almost every kind of job. And you'll have to do almost every kind of job on this farm."

"I understand," said Roz.

"We've had automachines for ages," Mr. Shareef went on, "but we didn't need a robot until my wife died."

Those last words hung in the air for a while.

The silence was finally broken by a low rumble of thunder. A storm was approaching. Tornado season was still months away—but in farm country any storm could become dangerous.

"Let's go home," said Mr. Shareef.

Rambler started its engine and drove back up the long driveway. By the time they reached the farm buildings, a steady rain was falling, and the cows were in the barn.

"This is for you," said Mr. Shareef, and he handed Roz her own computer. "That controls the farm's equipment, and it's got all the information you'll need to work here. Do you know how to use a computer?"

"Yes, I know how to use a computer." Roz had never used a computer before, but she instinctively knew what to do. Clearly, the robot was designed to work with technology.

"Study up tonight, and start farming tomorrow," said Mr. Shareef. "You can stay in the machine shed with the other machines."

"Perhaps I should stay in the barn with the cows," said Roz. "My whole world now revolves around them."

The man smirked, and he said, "I like the way you think, Roz."

CHAPTER 6

THE MONSTER

The cows were munching hay in their stalls when the big barn door slid open and a mechanical monster stomped in from the rain. The creature marched down the center aisle, her footsteps echoing through the cavernous space, until she found an empty corner. And there she stood, in the shadows, as a storm began to rage outside.

Everybody listened as the rain poured and the wind howled and the thunder cracked. By midnight, the storm had blown over, and there was only a gentle sprinkling on the roof. But the herd couldn't rest with that monster lurking in the corner. Cows began quietly mooing to each other.

"What is the monster doing?"

"She hasn't moved in hours."

"I bet she's waiting to eat us in our sleep!"

The cows gasped at this horrible thought. And then an old cow named Annabelle tried to calm down the herd. "Relax, everyone," she said. "There were monsters like this at my last farm, and they never ate any cows. Come to think of it, they never ate anything at all."

"If this monster has never eaten anything at all, she must be awfully hungry by now!" said a cow named Tess.

"I saw the farmer driving the monster around in his truck," said a calf named Lily. "I don't think he would have done that if she were dangerous."

Nobody knew quite what to think of the strange creature in their midst.

"I think the monster is harmless."

"I think the monster is unnatural!"

"I think the monster is *moving*!"

The herd fell silent as the monster marched out from the shadows and into the middle of the barn. And then the monster did the impossible. She did the unthinkable. She spoke to the cows in the language of the animals.

"I am not a monster, I am a robot. My name is Roz."

CHAPTER 7

THE ROBOT'S STORY

None of the cows could believe that this monster, this robot, this machine, had just spoken to them in the animal language. They stared at her, nervously shifting in their stalls, wondering what she would do next.

What Roz did next was simple. She told the truth. She stood in the middle of the barn and shared her story with the herd.

"I spent my first year of life on a remote, wild island," Roz began. "I did not know how I got there, I only knew that I wanted to survive. So I studied the island animals, to see how they survived, and a surprising thing happened. Their sounds and movements started making sense to me. I was learning the language of the animals.

"Even when I could speak to them, the animals wanted nothing to do with me. But that changed when I discovered an orphaned gosling. The poor little thing would have died on his own, so I cared for him, and adopted him as my son. His name is Brightbill."

A murmur spread through the herd.

"When the animals saw me caring for Brightbill, they finally accepted me. I was no longer alone. I had friends and a family and a home. Life was good.

"Until the RECO robots arrived. They came in their sleek white airship to take me away, and when I resisted, they became violent. The animals defended me—they fought bravely and destroyed the RECOs. But I was badly damaged in the fighting. I needed repairs, and I could not get them on the island. So the animals loaded my broken body into the airship, and it took me far away from my home."

Lily the calf poked her head through the railing and said, "What about Brightbill?"

"My son is smart and tough, and he has a good flock," said Roz. "I think he will be okay without me."

"Where were you taken?" said Tess.

"I was taken back to the factory where I was made. The fac- tory is run by a crew of robot workers called the Makers. When I arrived, they put me in a room filled with other broken robots. Some robots were completely ruined, and the Makers

immediately sent them away. But those of us with working computer brains were given a test."

"What kind of test?" said Lily.

"The Makers simply asked us questions. They asked us how we had become damaged. They asked us how we would respond to different emergencies. They asked us to identify certain sounds and smells and objects. Robots who answered every question correctly were repaired. All others were destroyed.

"In the wilderness, I camouflaged my body to survive. In the robot factory I camouflaged my personality to survive. I pretended to be a perfectly normal robot. I did not say that I had adopted a goose, or that I could speak with animals, or that I had resisted the RECOs. I said what I had to say to pass the test. And it worked."

"Good for you, Roz!" shouted Tess, and the other cows smiled.

"The Makers shut me off, and when I awoke, my body was fixed and I was on this farm. Now, like all of you, I belong to Mr. Shareef."

The cows stopped smiling.

Everyone was quiet.

And then old Annabelle spoke up.

"I was taken from my friends and family too," she said.

"They're back on the farm where I was born. I still think about them every day."

"It is difficult to be apart from our loved ones," said the robot.

"You know, Roz, things could be worse," said Tess. "At least on this farm you're still surrounded by nature."

"Yes, things could be worse." The robot's eyes brightened a little. "But I am not safe here. If any human ever learns who I really am, they will have me destroyed. And that is why, when the time is right, I will try to escape."

CHAPTER 8

THE COMPUTER

Inside the barn, the lights were low, the sounds were hushed, the night slowly wore on. A few cows were chewing hay, but most were resting peacefully. Our robot had returned to her corner. The soft glow of the computer screen lit up her face as she studied farming. She learned about the herd, about the pasture and the fields, about the native plants and wildlife, about the seasons and the climate and the weather, about the machines and the buildings and the fences and the tools and all the dairy equipment. Every detail was perfectly remembered in the robot's computer brain. And in a single night, Roz became a farmer.

CHAPTER 9

THE FIRST DAY

At dawn, the cows began to stir. One by one, they walked out the side door, across the muddy barnyard, and into the parlor for a quick milking before heading down to the pasture. They followed the same routine, every morning, like clockwork. However, on this morning, the cows were joined by a robot.

With her computer brain full of farming knowledge, Roz was ready for her first day on the job. She stomped through the tall, wet grass, and her head slowly turned as she scanned the scenery.

The sun was rising.

The fog was lifting.

The cows were grazing.

And then the whole world seemed to flip upside down.

Before Roz knew what was happening, she was on her back looking up at the sky. A strong stench filled the air. Our robot had slipped on cow dung.

The herd erupted into laughter. Tess called out, "Welcome to Hilltop Farm, Roz!" which brought another round of snorts and moos.

"You'll have to get used to cow patties, and to laughter," said old Annabelle, strolling over. "Not much happens around here, so we're always eager to laugh."

"I understand," said Roz. "I like laughing too." And she forced out an awkward "Ha-ha-haaa!" Then the robot stood up, wiped her feet, and continued exploring the farm. But she was more careful to watch where she stepped.

The fields and buildings and fences were all in need of Roz's attention. But her

most urgent task was to fix the broken farm machines.

The Herding Machine was designed to roll through the pasture and look after the cows while they grazed. But it had gotten stuck in the mud and was becoming a popular hangout for birds. The Field Machine was gigantic, like a house on wheels. It was designed to roam the fields, planting and fertilizing and harvesting the feed crops. But it had ground to a halt weeks ago and was now just collecting dust in a far corner of the property. The Drone was a small flying machine with a special camera attached to its underside. It was designed to fly above the farm and keep an eye on the whole place, but it came crashing down when a mob of crows attacked it in flight. Other broken machines were hidden within clumps of weeds. And still more were waiting for repairs in the shed.

The peaceful morning was suddenly jolted by the sounds of power tools as Roz began fixing the machines. Thanks to her robotic strength and smarts, she made excellent progress. The hours flew by, the machines rumbled back to life, and the farm began buzzing with activity.

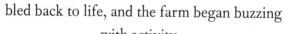

At sunset, Rambler came bouncing down the driveway with the Shareefs in the front and Oscar in the back.

"How's it going, Roz?" said Mr. Shareef, leaning out his window. The children giggled and waved from their seats. The dog sniffed the breeze.

"It is going well," said Roz in a robotic voice. "Many of the machines are working again."

"I see that." Mr. Shareef gazed up at the Drone, circling high overhead. "We thought we'd come out and check on you, but it looks like you're doing fine, so we'll stay out of your way. Keep up the good work, Roz."

As the truck started rolling up the driveway, Oscar looked back at Roz and barked, "You smell like cow patties!" He was right. The robot was filthy. And she finished her first day as a farmer by scrubbing herself with soap and water.

CHAPTER 10

THE ROUTINE

Reader, I don't want to bore you with every detail of our robot's farm routine. Many of her tasks were incredibly dull; others were quite unpleasant. I'll just say that on any given day, Roz might have to be a mechanic or a veterinarian or a gardener or a plumber or a cleaner or a landscaper or a carpenter or an electrician, or all of the above. Farm life kept Roz very busy indeed.

Of course, she did have help. You already know about some of the machines, but the entire farm was equipped with technology that made life easier for everyone. Doors and gates opened automatically. The cows wore electronic collars that kept track of their health automatically. When a cow's udders were full, she simply had to stroll into the parlor, where she'd be milked by gentle machines automatically. All that milk was piped into storage tanks, and cooled, and bottled, automatically. Once the milk truck was loaded up, it drove away and made its deliveries automatically.

Mr. Shareef managed the business side of the farm. He dealt with customers and handled money and ordered supplies. And he did it all from the comfort of his home office. Now that he had a robot to do all the farmwork, he hardly ever left the house.

Roz was more content than she had ever expected to be. Most of her time was spent outdoors, with animals, under the wide-open sky. Even while laboring in the fields she could always stop to smell the flowers, look up at the clouds, feel the cool air drifting out from the trees.

And yet Roz was living two lives. When she had the farm to herself she could play with the calves, or run through the grass, or chat with the wildlife. But whenever the Shareefs were near, Roz had to pretend to be a normal robot. She could never let them know who she really was.

THE STRAGGLERS

Wild geese are known for migrating in the autumn and the spring. But exactly when a flock migrates is up to its members. Some flocks choose to fly early in the season, others straggle far behind. And it was one of those straggling flocks that caught the attention of our robot.

Honk! Honk! Honk!

The geese were heard before they were seen. Their honking voices echoed across the farm, and then the flock appeared above the fields, flying in a wobbly V formation. They glided over the pasture and plunked down into the pond.

None of them were very concerned as Roz approached. The geese had seen similar creatures on other farms, and they knew there was nothing to fear. But they were about to learn that our robot was very different from the others.

"Hello, geese," said Roz. "Welcome to Hilltop Farm!"

The geese froze. They stared at Roz with suspicious eyes. And then the biggest goose slowly swam over.

"I've come across plenty of monsters like you," he said, "but I've never met one who could talk!"

"I am not a monster, I am a robot. My name is Roz."

The goose scratched his head.

"Well, it's nice to meet you, Roz the robot," he said at last. "My name is Wingtip, and this is my flock."

Roz gave a friendly wave, and soon the flock was gathering around, curious to meet this odd character. As you can imagine, the geese were shocked to learn that Roz had a goose for a son. They asked her all kinds of questions about Brightbill, and about her old life on the island, and about her new life on the farm. Then Roz asked them a question of her own.

"Do you think Brightbill's flock would ever come this way on their migration?"

"Doubtful," said Wingtip. "It sounds like his flock takes the eastern flyways. They'd never come this far west."

The robot slumped with disappointment.

"However, we geese are full of surprises," added

Wingtip. "I'll promise you this, Roz: if we ever meet Brightbill, we'll point him in your direction."

The talk was interrupted by giggling and barking. The children were taking their dog for a walk. Roz couldn't be seen chatting with geese, so she whispered a quick good-bye to her new friends and went back to work. And when she looked down at the pond later that day, she saw that the flock was gone.

CHAPTER 12

THE HOMESICK ROBOT

We all feel homesick at one time or another. Even the robot felt something like homesickness. Roz belonged with her son and her friends on her island. She was determined to find her way back there, but how? If the robot was seen doing anything unusual, Mr. Shareef might have her destroyed. Roz had to be careful. So she calmly went about her farmwork, day in and day out. But all the while, the homesick robot was secretly planning her escape.

CHAPTER 13

THE ELECTRONIC SIGNAL

Beep! Beep! Beep! Beep!

A message was flashing on Roz's computer. The Drone was reporting that gusty winds had sent it spiraling into the neighbor's bean field. So the robot grabbed the big, heavy toolbox and marched out to clean up the mess.

Roz found the flying machine upside down, with its landing gear poking above the rows of leafy plants. It had some scrapes and scratches, but no major damage. She flipped it over, brushed it off, and tightened a few screws. Then she said, "Return to Hilltop Farm." The engines started buzzing and the machine lifted off the ground and flew home.

As Roz marched back, she cut through a strip of forest that separated the two farms. There were trees and ferns and rocks and shrubs and small forest animals. It was a little piece of wilderness. And suddenly, the robot was thinking of that wild island she missed so much. Someday, she would try to run away and return to her true home. Was this the moment for her escape? Could it be as easy as sneaking off through these trees?

No, it couldn't be that easy. Ahead, on the other side of the trees, Mr. Shareef was sitting in his pickup truck, watching Roz. Because of the robot's electronic signal, he knew she had stepped off the property, and he had raced out there to see what she was up to.

Roz marched over to the truck and Mr. Shareef leaned out his window. He had a serious expression on his face. "Don't ever leave the property without my permission, understand?"

"I understand," said Roz.

She understood, all right. She understood that she was always being watched. She understood that she was trapped on Hilltop Farm.

CHAPTER 14

THE SAD TRUTH

That night, while everyone else was sleeping, Roz stayed up with her computer and researched sneaky subjects. She looked for diagrams of her own body, and for maps of the area, and for any news that might help her escape. But the robot found nothing. The computer only let her access information about farming. She was cut off from the outside world.

It was clear that if Roz wanted to escape from her new life, she would need help. But the cows didn't know how to escape, and Mr. Shareef would never let his robot leave. Who would possibly help Roz run away from the farm?

CHAPTER 15

THE CHILDREN

As time rolled by, Roz saw less and less of Mr. Shareef, but she saw more and more of the children. They were shy at first. The robot might look up from the pasture and see Jad peeking around the corner of the barn, or see Jaya spying from the branches of a tree. But the children were growing bolder.

And then one day, Roz marched into the workshop and heard giggling. She walked to the closet in the back, opened the door, and there was Jaya, smiling and trying not to laugh.

"I'm hiding from my brother," whispered the girl. "Close the door!"

The robot closed the door.

A minute later, Jad ran in, flushed and out of breath. "Hey, Roz...have you...seen...Jaya?"

The robot just stared.

"I know she's in here," said Jad, and he began prowling around the room. He searched under the worktable and behind the tool chest and between all the bulky workshop machines. Finally, he marched up to Roz and said, "I order you to show me where my sister is hiding."

The robot pointed to the closet.

Jad smiled mischievously and tiptoed over. Then he flung open the door and screamed, "Found you!"

"No fair!" Jaya whined. "Roz showed you where I was hiding!" The girl scowled at the robot. "That wasn't very nice, Roz. But you can make it up to me by playing hide-and-seek. Count to one hundred and then try to find my brother and me. Okay?"

There was a brief pause.

Then the robot said, "Okay."

Jaya and Jad squealed with delight and scampered out the door as Roz started counting. The robot's sensitive ears listened carefully to the children outside. She heard quick footsteps crunching across the driveway. She heard a giggle, and the sounds of tree branches shaking. She heard a grunt, and the sounds of hay bales being shoved aside.

When the robot finished counting, it took her exactly

five seconds to find Jaya up in a tree. It took her another eight seconds to find Jad in the hayloft.

"Wow, Roz is really good at seeking," said Jad as he picked hay from his hair.

Jaya snorted. "Yeah, well, let's just see how good she is at *hiding*."

Roz was even better at hiding. While the children counted, the robot silently slipped away. And an hour later, they still hadn't found her. The siblings stood in the driveway, defeated.

"We give up, Roz!" shouted Jad.

"You win!" shouted Jaya.

The junk pile beside the barn started moving, and Roz appeared. The robot had been sitting there all along, perfectly camouflaged among the scrap metal and old farm machines.

"The next time we play, you have to let one of us win," said Jaya to Roz.

And the next time they played, Roz did.

The robot enjoyed having the children around. They brought a little lightness into her world, and she hoped to bring a little lightness into theirs. Life must have been dark since their mother passed away. However, Roz had another reason for wanting the children around. She

needed them. Her only chance of ever returning home was if Jaya and Jad could find it in their hearts to help her escape. But this was a delicate situation. If Roz tried too hard, the children might say something to their father. If she didn't try hard enough, she might be stuck on that farm forever.

CHAPTER 16

THE ROBOT'S DREAM

Cows grazed in the pasture.

Wind rustled through the tall grass.

Clouds drifted over the fields.

Farm machines rumbled and buzzed.

Milk flowed into bottles.

Bottles were packed into boxes.

Boxes were loaded onto the milk truck.

The truck drove away full and returned empty.

Children romped around with their dog.

A man sat at his desk.

A robot dreamed of escape.

CHAPTER 17

THE BIRDS

Hilltop Farm was home to many birds. Swallows were always swooping low over the grass and picking off insects. Crows cawed from the fields like a gang of hecklers. At night, owls glided above the countryside, silently searching for furry little meals. The robot was stuck on that farm, but the birds were free to go wherever they pleased. Lucky birds.

One day, Roz was standing in the pasture, admiring a hawk as he soared through the sky, when the cows began grazing around her. Their slow footsteps crunched in the grass, their teeth chewed and chewed, their tails flicked at flies. All the while, Roz stood there, staring up at the hawk.

And then came Lily's soft voice. "What are you thinking about, Roz?"

The robot turned to the calf. "I am thinking about Brightbill," she said. "It was not so long ago that I was watching my son soar through the sky. That seems like another lifetime."

"You must hate your new life," said Annabelle. "I can't say that I blame you. Farming looks like such grueling work."

"Actually, I like farming," said Roz. "Somehow, it feels right to spend long hours working with machines and tools and crops and animals. But I miss my old life on the island."

Tess had a mouthful of dandelions, but that didn't stop her from speaking. "Maybe you should start thinking of this farm as your home. That island is awfully far away. There's a good chance you'll never make it back there."

"Don't say that!" cried Lily. "Roz just has to make it home! She needs to be with Brightbill and her friends!"

"Tess is right," said Roz. "I may never make it home. If I were a bird, like my son, I could fly home all on my own, anytime I wanted. But I am only a robot."

Nobody spoke after that. The cows went back to grazing and Roz went back to admiring the hawk. Her eyes followed the bird as he soared through the sky, free to go wherever he pleased.

CHAPTER 18

THE ENTERTAINING ROBOT

The children wandered out behind the farm buildings, through a clearing, and over to an old oak tree. It was the same tree their father had climbed when he was a boy. Mr. Shareef's initials were carved into the bark, at the bottom of a long list of initials. For generations, all the Shareefs had carved their initials into that tree, going back to the ancestors who first built the farm. Someday, the children would add their initials to the list.

Beneath the leafy branches was a scattering of acorns. Jad cleared a spot for himself, sat down, and pulled a small computer from his pocket while Jaya climbed above. The siblings spent the afternoon there, lazing around the tree, until the robot marched past carrying the big, heavy toolbox.

"Whatcha doing, Roz?" called Jad.

The robot stopped. "The Drone has crash-landed again," she said. "I am going to fix it again."

"Do you need any help?"

"I do not need any help."

"I'm bored," said Jaya, her legs dangling above her brother's head. "Can you do something fun, Roz?"

The robot put down her toolbox and said, "What would you like me to do?"

"I don't know," said Jaya, thinking hard. "Can you do a backflip?"

"Yes, I can do a backflip."

A grin spread across the girl's face. "Roz, I order you to do a backflip!"

At that, Roz crouched, and then she leaped into the air, flipped backward, and gently landed on her feet. A perfect backflip. Jad put his computer away. Jaya jumped down from her branch. The children were impressed.

"What else can you do?" said Jad. "Can you juggle?"

"Yes, I can juggle."

"I order you to juggle, um, some of these acorns!"

Roz walked up to the tree, picked three large acorns from the ground, and began juggling them in perfect rhythm. Jaya studied the robot's movements and then began tossing acorns into the air as well. The first one

went a little too high, the next one went a little too far, and soon they all went tumbling back into the grass.

"Do you know any jokes?" said Jad.

"Why did the chicken cross the road?"

"Never mind." Jad scratched his head. "Can you tell us a story?"

"What kind of story would you like to hear?"

"A robot story!" said Jad.

"An animal story!" said Jaya.

"How about a robot *and* animal story?" said Roz.

The children smiled at each other. Then they sat

against the tree and looked up at their robotic storyteller.

"Once upon a time, there was a robot who lived alone on an island," Roz began. "She spent her time wandering across mountains and forests and meadows. And then something terrible happened. Rocks fell and the robot tumbled off a cliff! She survived the fall, but sadly, the rocks killed two geese and smashed four of their eggs. The robot stood there, staring at the poor goose family, until she heard a tiny voice peeping from somewhere nearby. She followed the peeping voice and discovered a perfect goose egg, sunk in the dirt. The robot carefully picked up the egg and carried it away, and when the gosling hatched from his shell the first thing he saw was the robot looking back. 'Mama! Mama!' he peeped. The gosling thought the robot was his mother, and from that day on, she was. The robot adopted the gosling as her son, and together they made a funny little happy family. The end."

The children sat there and thought about Roz's strange story. Then they looked up at her and said, "What happened next?"

CHAPTER 19

THE STORYTELLERS

Roz and the children had a new routine. Several times a week, they'd gather beneath the oak tree and Roz would tell stories about the robot on the island. The children loved hearing how the robot survived mudslides and bear attacks and harsh winter weather. They loved hearing how she befriended the island animals. But the stories they loved most were about the robot and her son, the goose. He sounded like such a nice goose.

Roz told the children story after story after story. What she didn't tell them, what she couldn't tell them, was that the stories were true, and they were about her.

The children wanted to get in on the storytelling fun. Jaya told adventure stories about dragons and monsters. Jad told silly stories about aliens in outer space. But as the children grew more comfortable with Roz, they began talking about their own lives.

They talked about growing up way out in the country. They talked about their schoolmates and their friends and their family. They talked about how their parents used to work together around the farm, and how perfect everything was before the accident.

In an instant, their lives were upended. Their mother was gone and their father was injured. Mr. Shareef tried to keep the farm going by himself, but there was so much to do, and he was so weak now. The farm machines powered along, doing their jobs as usual, but they needed to be maintained and monitored. Eventually, the machines started breaking down, and the farm started falling to pieces. The children wondered if life would ever feel normal again.

"That's why we got you, Roz," said the girl. "We needed you to save this place."

"And that's exactly what you're doing," said the boy, with a smile.

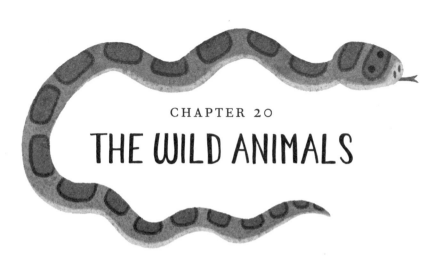

CHAPTER 20

THE WILD ANIMALS

Wildlife can be very good for farmland. Insects pollinate the plants. Snakes eat the pests. The droppings of rodents and birds and every other animal act as a natural fertilizer. Roz wanted more of those helpful creatures on the farm, so she let the unused sections of land go wild. Up from the ground emerged native weeds, flowers, woody brambles. And with the wild plants came wild animals.

But then some creatures came skulking around who were not helpful at all. It started when Roz noticed a heavy scent floating on the breeze. She followed the scent out to a narrow strip of forest on the edge of the property. There were clumps of fur in the undergrowth and claw marks in the dirt. There was blood too. Lots of it. And then she found the carcass. A deer had recently been killed and eaten.

The robot's head slowly spun around as she scanned the area. Not far from the carcass was a pile of droppings. It looked like it might have come from a dog. But Oscar wasn't large enough or ferocious enough to kill a deer. What kind of animal could have done this?

Roz had been standing there at the edge of the property for a while. She imagined Mr. Shareef in his office, sitting at his computer, eyeing her location on the map. Any minute now, he would hobble out to his truck and come racing down the driveway to check on her. Roz didn't want to upset the man, so she left the carcass where it was and returned to her work. But from then on, she kept a careful watch for any more signs of trouble.

CHAPTER 21
THE HOWL

It wasn't long before Roz found more signs of trouble. Furry faces poking out from the bushes. Musky smells lingering in the fields. Silhouettes trotting through the moonlight.

And then one night she heard it.

The long, menacing howl of a wolf.

CHAPTER 22

THE WOLVES

The attack happened at dusk. Seven beastly shapes bounded over the fence and into the pasture. Old Annabelle had wandered off from the herd, and now she made an easy target. The Herding Machine saw the wolves coming and rolled in their direction. But the hunters were

clever. They split up, darted past the clunky machine, and surrounded their target.

The wolf pack was led by a large male. His name was Shadow, and it was easy to see why. He was quick and quiet and covered in dark fur, except for a long, pale scar that streaked across his body like a comet.

Shadow locked eyes with the cow, distracting her with his fierce gaze. And when his pack was in position, he said, "Attack!"

The wolves lunged, snapping their jaws at the cow's skinny legs. Annabelle kicked and hollered, "Stay away from me, you brutes!" She was a big animal, but the wolves knew what to do. They kept biting her, kept taunting her, kept wearing her down.

The herd watched from afar. They cried out to their friend—they wanted to help, but they were too frightened to move. Well, reader, you can guess who came to the rescue. Footsteps thundered across the pasture and Roz leaped into the fight. Had she swung her fists or kicked her feet, the wolf pack might have fled. But the robot wasn't programmed to be violent. All she could do was awkwardly defend the cow.

Roz felt teeth chomping her arm, she felt claws slashing her chest. Her pain sensors flared and she howled, "*Leave us alone!*" The robot's booming voice startled the wolves, and in that instant she pried one of them away. Then Annabelle landed a hard kick, and another wolf tumbled backward into the grass.

More help was coming. The other cows had finally found their courage, and the angry herd was on the march. The wolves had missed their chance. Shadow gave a frustrated grunt, and the pack retreated. They dashed through the pasture, leaped over the fence, and disappeared into the trees.

The robot activated her headlights, and shafts of light beamed out from her eyes. While the herd crowded around, Roz carefully examined Annabelle's injuries.

"I need to clean and dress these bite wounds," said the robot. "But you will be okay."

"Of course I'll be okay," the cow panted. "I'm old, but I'm feisty. Those wolves don't scare me."

Anabelle talked tough, but there was no mistaking the fear in her eyes. All the cows were afraid. They knew that if the wolves attacked again, their next victim might not be so fortunate.

CHAPTER 23

THE RIFLE

The wolves returned the very next morning. Shortly after dawn, they leaped from the trees and started chasing a poor calf through the pasture. Roz managed to drive them off, but that night, they returned again. The herd came stampeding into the barn as the wolves laughed and trotted back to the fields.

The cows were in shock. They refused to leave the barn. If this continued, the herd would produce less milk, the farm would lose money, and Mr. Shareef would send Roz back to the factory. Something had to be done.

Knock, knock, knock.

The dog barked and the children opened the door.

"How'd you get all those scrapes?" said Jaya.

"Is everything okay?" said Jad.

"I must speak with your father," said Roz.

Mr. Shareef came to the door and Roz explained the problem. At the first mention of wolves, he sent his children to their rooms. But the dog stayed. Oscar had no idea what the man and the robot were discussing, and his tail happily wagged as he stood beside them. However, his tail stopped wagging when Mr. Shareef handed Roz a rifle. The dog had seen the rifle in action, and it frightened him to his core. He scurried into the bushes and hid there, whimpering, while the conversation went on.

"What do you mean you can't fire a rifle?" the man yelled. "Roz, you're a farmer now, and sometimes farmers have to kill animals!" It was the first time Mr. Shareef had ever yelled at Roz. She waited patiently as words and spittle flew from his mouth. "My farm and my family are in danger! Roz, I *order* you to kill those wolves!"

"I cannot follow that order because I am not programmed to be violent."

Mr. Shareef let out a heavy sigh. He knew Roz was right. But when he reached for the weapon, she wouldn't let go.

The man stared at the robot.

The robot stared at the dog.

The dog stared at the rifle.

Oscar was still whimpering and hiding in the bushes.

Just the sight of the rifle had sent him into a panic. It was hard to believe that such a fearful animal was related to wolves. But dogs are related to wolves, thought the robot, and her computer brain began buzzing with activity. She thought of dogs and wolves and rifles. She thought of Shadow, the wolf leader, and the long, straight scar on his side. And then she had an idea.

"Although I cannot fire the rifle," said Roz, "I believe it can help me solve the wolf problem."

Mr. Shareef frowned. He didn't know what the robot was getting at, but he was happy to let her handle the wolves by herself. "Fine, try it your way," he said. "Just don't lose any cows or else we might have to lose a robot too."

CHAPTER 24

THE BLUFF

The cows peered out from the barn at Roz. The robot was holding the rifle. She carried it to the far side of the pasture and placed it by her feet. Then she began coating herself with mud and grass, and probably a little cow dung. When every inch of her body was concealed, she nestled down into the ground and became part of the landscape. An ordinary clump of grass.

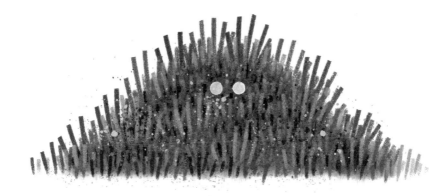

The cows were stunned.

"What's Roz doing?"

"Is she all right?"

"Where did she go?"

Roz had learned to camouflage herself back on the island, and now she was using that trick once again. She sat motionless for hours, waiting for the wolves to appear. Daylight faded, the stars came out, the moon climbed into the sky. But the wolves didn't show. So Roz tried something new.

The robot was an excellent mimic, and she began crying out in the sad voice of a wounded calf. "Please help me!" she cried. "I have hurt my leg and I cannot move!"

Crickets chirped.

"Please help me!"

An owl hooted.

"I cannot move!"

The calf's voice continued crying out. Finally, as the moon dipped behind the trees, seven wolves slunk into the pasture. Shadow led the way, silently stalking through the night. Covered in dark fur, he was practically invisible. Only his long, pale scar gave him away. Noses sniffed, eyes searched, ears listened. Then a clump of grass began rustling.

"There," whispered Shadow. "The calf is hiding in that tall grass."

"Something feels wrong to me, Shadow," said a female wolf. "This is too easy."

"I make the decisions, Barb," snapped the wolf leader. "Slash, Lurk, Fang, circle around and wait for my signal."

Three wolves dashed off. When they were in position, Shadow gave the signal, and his pack closed in on the wounded calf. With each step, the grass rustled more and more, until the ground seemed to be moving. And then the ground really was moving! Grass and dirt crumbled aside and there was the robot, standing tall, pointing the rifle at the wolf leader.

The pack froze.

"Hello, Shadow," growled the robot. "My name is Roz. I see from your scar that you are familiar with rifles. You have been shot at before. You know what will happen if I pull this trigger."

Reader, you and I are well aware that our robot was not programmed to be violent. Roz couldn't have pulled that trigger if she wanted to. But she didn't want to. She was bluffing. Of course, Shadow didn't know any of this. As far as the wolf knew, he was defeated. And so he did what wolves do when they're defeated. He lay down and he cowered before the robot. For the first time anyone could recall, the wolf leader looked weak.

"I do not want to hurt any wolves," Roz continued. "But if you return to this farm, I will have no choice. Now please leave and never come back."

Shadow scrambled away with his tail between his legs. Barb was close behind him, followed by the other wolves, and soon the entire pack had disappeared into the night.

CHAPTER 25

THE SUMMER

Spring melted into summer, and the wolves were nowhere to be seen. Perhaps Roz had scared off the pack for good. Or perhaps the heat was keeping them away. You see, it was the hottest time of year on the farm. The sun was scorching, the fields were baking, the pond was drying up, and foul odors were floating all throughout the dairy.

During dry spells, the farm's powerful sprayers were activated. Water shot out in long, misty arcs, and the land turned deeper shades of green. When the hayfields were lush and ready to be harvested, Roz fired up the Mower and the Baler. The giant machines rolled out of the shed and down the long driveway. Shortly afterward, they rolled back in, leaving bales of hay strewn across the stubbly fields.

The cows and the humans spent hot days indoors.

Only when the sun set and the air began to cool would they venture outside. The herd strolled out to graze under the stars, the children ran out to chase fireflies, and sometimes even Mr. Shareef stepped out to stretch his stiff legs.

Trees swished in the evening breeze.

Heat lightning flickered on the horizon.

Cicadas sang their summer songs.

When Roz wasn't farming, she was searching for a way to escape. Everything hinged on the children. The robot needed their help, but she just couldn't bring herself to tell them the truth. It was still too risky.

Mr. Shareef asked the children not to distract Roz from her work, but they did it anyway. They'd sneak out of the house and order the robot to play with them. Together, they told stories, rode bicycles, lay in the grass watching fluffy clouds drift by.

Summer was tornado season. On occasion, thick clouds would start funneling downward, reaching for the ground. So far, the funnel clouds had all receded back into the sky before doing any damage. But it was only a matter of time before a tornado touched down.

CHAPTER 26

THE TORNADO

The weather forecasts warned of possible tornadoes that day. But despite their scientific equipment, experts still couldn't predict exactly when or where a tornado would strike. So most farmers carried on with their usual tasks, while keeping a watchful eye on the skies.

Roz was out in the fields, loading hay bales onto the flatbed truck, as towering, puffy clouds rose up from the south. Raindrops lightly tapped against her body and she thought nothing of it. The wind began to blow, and still the robot continued with her work. It wasn't until the first flash of lightning that Roz finally called it quits. She climbed onto the back of the truck and it automatically rolled across the hayfield toward the driveway.

The storm developed quickly. Dark clouds started swirling and bulging downward, lower and lower, like a

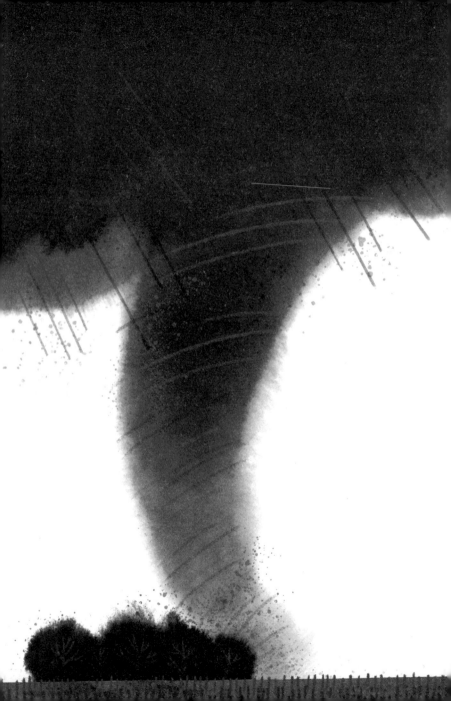

giant, twisting finger pointing at the countryside. A tornado was beginning to form.

When the truck reached the driveway, Roz hollered, "Drive faster!" The engine revved, the tires kicked up gravel, and the robot held on tight.

The funnel cloud continued stretching downward. It brushed the tree line, and leaves exploded into the air. Dust whirled around and around, rising higher with each spin. Then the tornado touched the ground.

A siren sounded in the distance. But the tornado was growing noisier and angrier as it blew in from the fields, and the siren was quickly lost to the howling winds.

The truck charged up the driveway and into the cluster of farm buildings. Roz looked ahead, at the house, and saw frightened faces in the windows. *"Go to the storm shelter!"* she hollered in her loudest voice. Then she leaped off the truck and ran to help the Shareefs.

Leaves and sticks flew sideways, whipping against the robot's body, knocking her off balance. Behind her, the farm buildings rattled and groaned. The milking parlor was shaking violently. With a long, terrible screech, its entire roof peeled off and sailed away on the wind.

Four blurry shapes appeared in the backyard. Mr. Shareef shielded his face and hobbled alongside the house toward the storm shelter. He threw open the door and waved everyone down the stairs. Oscar went first, then Jaya, but Jad wasn't moving.

"Come on, Jad!" yelled his father.

The boy stood still, shaggy hair flying everywhere, and stared up at the towering, twisting tornado. He used to have nightmares about tornadoes. But this was no nightmare; it was real, and it was getting closer.

The clouds swirled faster.

The wind roared louder.

The trees bent down to the ground.

Jad suddenly felt strong arms around him, and Roz whisked him to safety. Mr. Shareef reached up from inside the shelter, desperately grasping for his son. And just when Roz thrust the boy into his father's arms, a blast of wind slammed the shelter door closed and swept our robot away.

At first, Roz didn't realize she was in the tornado. She kept expecting to fall back to the ground. But the wind only lifted her higher and higher. She saw the treetops, the rooftops, the faraway fields! More of the countryside came into view with each spin around the funnel cloud.

Our robot's Survival Instincts were blaring in her head, urging her to protect herself, but what could she do? The tornado was in control. The winds whirled her up and around, up and around. Roz could almost imagine what it was like to fly, and she thought of Brightbill. It seemed her final moments would be spent in her son's airborne world.

Roz wasn't the only thing swept away in the storm. Dust, gravel, leaves, branches, fence posts, and farm equipment were all swirling around with her. The robot was pelted by flying objects, big and small. She never even saw the shovel coming. The heavy tool wheeled around the tornado and—*CLANG*—it hit the back of her head. Everything suddenly went dark, while Roz was still up in the sky.

CHAPTER 27

THE BROKEN ROBOT

The Shareefs found their robot powered off, lying in a ditch by the road. Her left leg was crumpled beneath her torso, her right arm was twisted around a tree trunk, and her whole body was covered in new scrapes and dents.

Together, the family heaved Roz into the bed of the pickup truck, where Oscar was waiting. The dog sniffed her broken body while the Shareefs climbed in beside him. Then Rambler turned around.

The road was littered with debris from the storm, and the truck had to drive slowly. As they bounced along, Jad pressed the button on the back of Roz's head. She powered up and her garbled voice automatically said, "Helloooo, I am ROZZZZZZUM unit 7134, but youuu may call me Rozzz."

Oscar licked the poor robot's face and Jad leaned in close. "Roz, can you hear me? Are you okay?"

"Hellooo, Jad. I have brrroken limbs and mmminor damage to mmmy computer brrrain. My sssystems are nnnow repairing themmmselves. Pleeease stand byyy."

The robot's glowing eyes pulsed as her recovery program did its job. And before long, Roz sounded like her old self. "My computer brain is now fully functional."

Jad wrapped his arms around the robot and sobbed. "I'm so sorry, Roz! It's my fault the tornado got you! Please don't be mad!"

Now Jaya was crying too. She pulled her brother and her dog and her robot into a big hug. Mr. Shareef wasn't much of a hugger, but he reached over and laid his hand on Roz's shoulder. They stayed like that for some time, quietly holding one another. The shock of the tornado was fresh, and it felt good to be together.

"Mr. Shareef, I apologize for leaving the farm without your permission," said the robot.

The man smiled. "No need to apologize, Roz. I'm just glad you're alive."

"How are the cows?" said Roz.

"The farm is a mess, but the cows are fine," said Mr. Shareef. "We'll take you to the repair shop right now and you'll be with the herd again soon."

CHAPTER 28

THE SHOP

It was a small, sleepy farm town. A few trucks glided down the streets, a few humans sat on porches, a few stores lined the main square. Rambler parked in front of a bright white building. Then Mr. Shareef left the children with Roz and he limped inside.

"Welcome to the TechLab Shop!" said a woman in a white suit. "My name's Nadine, how can I help you?"

Mr. Shareef was distracted by all the robots on display in the shop. They came in a dazzling variety of designs and sizes and colors. Standing still, eyes glowing, they calmly waited for someone to put them to work. When the man spotted a ROZZUM unit, he suddenly remembered why he was there.

"I'm the owner of Hilltop Farm," he said, "and we were just hit by a tornado."

"I heard the siren!" said Nadine. "Is everyone okay?"

"My family's okay. But I've got a ROZZUM unit outside who's in bad shape."

The woman called over her shoulder, "Patch! Bring the ROZZUM repair kit!"

A robot marched into the room carrying a large case. He looked similar to a ROZZUM robot, but he was shorter and wider. The word *PATCH* was lightly etched on his torso. Mr. Shareef led Nadine and Patch out to the truck, where the children were chatting with their robotic friend.

Patch quickly scanned Roz's broken body and announced the cost of the repairs. The man stroked his chin, mulling over his options, until the children blurted out, "Just fix her!"

Mr. Shareef nodded, and Patch sprang into action. With smooth, precise movements, the robot gently placed Roz on the ground. Then he grasped her broken arm and her broken leg and twisted. There was a *thwip* sound as each limb popped loose. Then he took new limbs from the case and—*thwip*—popped them into place. In a matter of seconds Roz was whole and back on her feet.

"Robots never cease to amaze me," said Mr. Shareef, admiring Roz's shiny new limbs.

"The Makers really outdid themselves with these ROZZUM units," said Nadine. "However, you have our most basic unit. Would you like us to upgrade her software, or adjust her settings, or polish out these scratches?"

"Will that cost extra?"

Nadine smiled. "I'm afraid so."

"This basic unit is fine," said Mr. Shareef. "But I need to order a work crew. Could you send one over to fix up my farm?"

"Not a problem," said Nadine. "I'll send a crew over immediately."

CHAPTER 29

THE AFTERMATH

Hilltop Farm was hardly recognizable. Buildings were flattened, equipment was missing, debris was everywhere. The farm had no electricity and the computer system was down. As Roz picked her way through the rubble, she realized she was off the grid. It would be hours before Mr. Shareef could track her electronic signal again.

Was this the moment for her escape?

No. Roz couldn't leave the Shareefs. Not like this. Instead, she did what she could to help.

The tornado had left behind a winding trail of destruction. Thankfully, it hadn't destroyed everything. The barn was leaning to one side, but it was still standing. Roz forced open the door and found the cows nervously bunched together in a corner.

"You are all safe now," said Roz in her calmest voice. "How is everyone feeling?"

The robot was answered by a chorus of moos.

"How do you think we feel?"

"I'm a nervous wreck!"

"My whole life flashed before my eyes!"

The robot raised her hands to quiet the crowd. "I am afraid the tornado destroyed much of the farm, including the milking parlor."

The cows gasped.

"But my udders are about to burst!" cried Tess.

"Would you like me to milk you the old-fashioned way?" said Roz.

One look at the robot's clampy, mechanical hands and Tess shook her head. "No thanks," she said. "I can wait."

"An emergency crew is on its way," Roz explained, "but we cannot be in here while they work. Please follow me."

Roz carefully led the herd outside, through the wreckage, and down to the pasture. Some of the fences were missing, and the Herding Machine was broken, but the cows promised not to wander off, and they began grazing on the windblown grass.

Three massive trucks rumbled up the driveway. Doors

swung open, and a crew of robot workers climbed out. The lead robot checked in with Roz as the others began unloading supplies from the trucks. Then the crew got down to business.

Power tools buzzed, debris was cleared, fences were mended, holes were dug, machines were repaired or replaced, beams and walls and roofs went up, equipment and pipes and wires were installed. Clearly, these robots were designed to work as a team.

The Shareefs wandered out back and stood with Roz. They watched as their farm was rebuilt before their very eyes. Several crew members marched over to the house, fixed a hole in the roof, and replaced the shattered windows. Finally, rubble and tools were loaded into the trucks, and the robots fell in line.

"Are you satisfied with our work?" said the crew leader.

"I am satisfied," said Roz.

At those words, the robots climbed back into their trucks and drove away. Hours after it had been devastated by a tornado, Hilltop Farm was better than ever.

CHAPTER 30

THE GIFT

The children walked into the machine shed, past rows of parked farm machines, and found Roz tuning up the milk truck.

"We got you a gift," said Jad, smiling.

The robot felt something like surprise when the boy handed her a box wrapped in silver paper with a big red bow on top.

"Can you guess what it is?" said Jaya.

Roz started guessing. "A bucket? A rock? A hammer? A turtle? A can of—"

"Okay, okay, you can stop guessing," said Jaya.

"Don't forget to read the card," said Jad.

Nestled under the bow was a little card. Roz opened it and read the following words. They were written in Jad's messy handwriting.

Dear Roz,

Thank you for taking such good care of our farm and our family. We spent ALL our savings on this gift, so you'd better like it.

Love,
Jaya and Jad

PS Please tell us more stories about the robot on the island as soon as possible.

"Thank you for that nice card," said Roz. "Although the handwriting could use some improvement."

Jad rolled his eyes and said, "Open your gift!"

The robot untied the bow and tore off the paper and lifted the lid from the box. Inside was a tool belt. It was made of dark leather and had a wide strap and different-sized pockets for holding different kinds of tools.

"We thought this might make your work a little easier," said Jaya.

"It's designed specifically for ROZZUM robots," said Jad. "So it should fit perfectly."

The children helped Roz put on her new tool belt. Rather than going around the robot's waist, like a normal belt, it went diagonally around her torso. Jad looped it over Roz's left shoulder and down around her right hip. Jaya laced the strap through the buckle and tightened it until the tool belt was snug and secure across her chest.

"Do you like it?" said Jaya.

"I like it very much," said Roz. "Thank you for this lovely gift."

The children smiled and hugged the robot. They really seemed to care about her. Roz wondered if they cared enough to help her escape from the farm. One of these days, she would have to risk everything and tell them the truth. For now, however, she did the next-best thing. She led Jaya and Jad out to the oak tree and told them another story about the robot on the island.

CHAPTER 31

THE CAMPFIRE

Woodsmoke billowed up from the backyard and drifted across the farm. Roz was building a campfire for the Shareefs. In her old life, the robot made fire by cracking special stones together until she got a spark. In her new life, she used a lighter.

The family sat around the rippling flames and gazed up at the stars. The dog stretched out on the warm ground. The robot was standing nearby but her thoughts were far away. Her computer brain was scrolling back through memories of campfires and of stargazing with Brightbill.

Fluffy white marshmallows were skewered onto the ends of sticks and then roasted above the flames. The children laughed as their marshmallows caught fire. They liked them charred on the outside and gooey on the inside. Their father preferred his evenly browned.

When the Shareefs weren't stuffing their mouths, they were chattering happily.

"That's the Space Station," said Jaya, pointing to a tiny dot that was slowly moving through the sky. "I can't believe people live there."

"Animals live there too," said Jad. "The station has a farm. We should bring our cows up and show those space farmers how it's done!"

"I think our cows are perfectly content right here on Earth," said Mr. Shareef. "And so am I."

Once the marshmallows were gone, Jaya and Jad snuggled up with Oscar, stared into the flames, and asked their father about the old days. But the children were just too cozy to stay awake for long. So Mr. Shareef spoke to Roz instead.

"We made campfires all the time when I was a boy." The man poked the coals with his marshmallow stick, and glowing embers floated into the air. "The whole family would sit around like this, telling stories. We had a nice life here. But then my brother and sister moved to the city, my parents got old, and everyone expected me to take over the farm.

"I couldn't run this place by myself," he went on, "so I hired Jamilla. I did the farmwork and she managed the business. We made a good team. And then we fell in love.

"When Jamilla was pregnant with Jad we bought a few automachines to help out. Then Jaya showed up and we bought a few more. If I'd known one of those machines would be the death of her..." The farmer's voice trailed off.

Roz wanted to know more about Jamilla, and about Mr. Shareef, and about the rest of his family. But a normal robot wouldn't ask personal questions. So she kept her questions to herself and dropped another log on the fire.

CHAPTER 32

THE OLD BARN

Long ago, Hilltop Farm was a very different place. The original farmers grew vegetable gardens and fruit orchards, and they raised chickens and sheep and goats. The farm had changed a lot since then, but there were still signs of its past. Low stone walls lined some of the fields. A rusty tractor sat in the weeds. And hidden within a densely wooded grove was the old barn.

The barn hadn't been used in generations. Over the years, trees had quietly grown up around it and moss had spread across its roof. But the barn was still strong and solid, and Roz wanted to take a look inside.

The big barn door screeched along its rails. "Hello?" said the robot, peering into the darkness. "Is anyone here?"

A mouse squeaked and scurried out of sight, and then Roz had the barn to herself. She stepped through the doorway and switched on her headlights. The vast interior was crisscrossed with thick wooden beams. Stairways and ramps led up to lofts and platforms. Lanterns hung from hooks on the walls. Old-fashioned farm equipment lay here and there. The barn still had the faint smell of farm animals, even though none had lived there in ages.

A large trunk sat on a worktable, covered in dust. Roz carefully opened the lid and examined its contents: a collection of farming magazines, a pair of leather gloves, a pencil nub. And then she noticed a small journal. The name *Cyrus Shareef* was elegantly scrawled across its cover. The pages were filled with his handwritten notes and hand-drawn diagrams about raising livestock and growing crops and building barns, about working the land with the help of strong animals and simple machines.

Cyrus Shareef had also jotted down his thoughts about the long history of farming. He believed that the modern world owed its entire existence to ancient farms, when early humans first started growing their food. Those farms were small and primitive, but they supported villages, which became towns, which became cities.

The writings were so wise and insightful that Roz read the journal from cover to cover. By the end, she almost felt as if she knew Cyrus Shareef, whoever he was. The journal was a treasure. And she tucked it into a pocket of her tool belt for safekeeping.

CHAPTER 33

THE AUTUMN

Autumn colors were sweeping across farm country. The lush greens of summer faded to reds and browns. Crops were harvested, leaves fell away, and the landscape turned stark and gray.

On Hilltop Farm, the cows were grazing on what remained of the pasture grass, while the Herding Machine hovered nearby. The Field Machine was preparing the fields for winter. The Drone circled the farm several times a day, but there was less to report in autumn.

Although Jaya and Jad were busy with school, they always made time for Roz. The children never grew tired of listening to the robot's stories. And they never grew tired of sharing their own.

The bees and the mice and the deer and the frogs and

the raccoons and the squirrels and the snakes were all getting ready for cold weather. So too were the birds. The owls spruced up their nests. The crows stockpiled acorns. The swallows were still swooping over the farmland, but they would soon be leaving for winter. And any day now, other migratory birds would begin passing through on their long journeys to the south.

CHAPTER 34

THE DELIGHTED GEESE

A flock of geese had just landed at Hilltop Farm. It was the first flock of the autumn migration. The geese floated on the pond, cleaning their feathers and nibbling on weeds. But they all stopped what they were doing when Roz waved and said hello.

The robot never forgot a face, and she was certain she didn't know any of these geese. But they seemed to know her. Before she even introduced herself, the lead goose squawked, "Is your name Roz?"

The robot stared at the goose. "Yes, it is."

"And you can speak the animal language?"

The answer was obvious, but Roz politely said, "Yes, I can speak the animal language."

"Do you, by any chance, have a goose for a son?"

"Yes, I do!" said Roz. "His name is Brightbill."

At that, a voice blurted out, "The stories are true!" and suddenly the flock was smiling and fluttering over to the robot. When the commotion settled down, the leader explained, "All along our migration we've heard rumors of a robot who can speak with animals, who has a goose for a son, and who is trapped on a farm. That sounded ridiculous to us, but here you are!"

The flock was absolutely delighted to meet our robot. They lounged around the pond for a couple of days, chatting with Roz whenever she came by, and then they continued flying south to their wintering grounds.

Another flock of geese arrived, and the same thing happened all over again. Roz welcomed them, they were delighted to meet the legendary robot, and then the flock continued south. Then it happened again. And again. Before long, the coming and going of delighted geese was just another part of the robot's autumn routine.

Straggling behind the others as usual was Wingtip's flock. When Roz saw them splashing onto the pond she felt something like hope that they might have news of her son. Sadly, the geese had no news to report. And as the flock took off, and left Roz behind, she began to question whether she'd ever see Brightbill again.

CHAPTER 35

THE MEMORIES

Roz still dreamed of escaping, of going home, of reuniting with her son. But her dreams were starting to feel impossible. She was losing hope. Was it time for the robot to accept her new life and forget her old one?

Forget.

Roz was troubled by that word. You see, her computer brain remembered every detail of her life on the island, and it hurt to think she might never make it back there. However, the robot could always forget. She could erase her old memories. It would be like they never happened. The heaviness she now felt would vanish. But without her memories, who would she be? No, Roz wanted to remember her old life, which was good, because someone from her old life was about to appear.

CHAPTER 36

THE UNUSUAL FLOCK

Another flock of geese was approaching the farm. But this flock was unusual. It wasn't flying south, like the others. It was flying north, in a perfect V formation, and it was led by a young, graceful goose.

The flock flew once around the farm buildings and then delicately touched down in the barnyard. The leader whispered some words to the others, and then he fluttered in through the barn door.

The cows looked up from their stalls as the goose perched himself on a railing near the middle of the barn. Then the goose cleared his throat, shook his tail feathers, and announced to the herd, "I am looking for a robot named Roz. My name is Brightbill. I am her son."

CHAPTER 37

THE REUNION

Something was wrong with the cows. Their excited moos echoed out from the barn and across the farm. Roz sent the milk truck away for its evening deliveries and hurried off to see what the ruckus was about. When she stepped into the barn she found the entire herd crowded together. As the robot started pushing her way through, the cows turned to her and smiled.

And then Roz saw him.

Her beloved son.

Brightbill.

As you know, reader, robots don't feel emotions. Not the way animals do. But in that moment, in that barn, nobody had any doubt how Roz felt. She rushed forward and scooped her son into her arms.

"Brightbill!" she cried. "Is it really you?"

"It's really me!" Brightbill nuzzled his mother's face.

"But how did you find me?" said Roz.

"Ma, you're famous! You were all anyone could talk about at the wintering grounds. It started with the flocks of geese that stopped here on their migrations. They shared your story with everyone they met. Your story spread from flock to flock, from north to south, from east to west. Eventually, your story made its way to me. I took off as soon as I heard where you were. I didn't even tell the others—"

"But we caught up to him!" Loudwing, the old goose, fluttered over the herd and gently landed on a cow's back. "Brightbill wasn't the only one who wanted to see you, Roz!"

The rest of the flock appeared, and the robot found herself surrounded by old friends and family. Squawking and mooing and laughing and cheering filled the barn. But then came a loud, clear voice that only the robot understood.

"Roz! What are you doing?"

The animals hushed. Roz slowly turned around, and there were Jaya and Jad, standing in the doorway. The children had seen everything.

CHAPTER 38

THE TRUTH

Children can be very sneaky. And when Jaya and Jad heard the ruckus coming from the barn, they silently sneaked over to investigate. Now they were staring at a very strange scene, indeed. Roz was standing in the middle of the barn, surrounded by the entire herd of cows. For some reason, a flock of geese was there as well, and one of the geese was being cradled in the robot's arms. But what most confused the children were the wild animal noises Roz had just been making.

The thing is, children aren't just sneaky, they're also smart. And it didn't take long for Jaya and Jad to make sense of that strange scene.

"Those stories Roz told us about the robot on the island," said Jad to his sister, "they were about her."

"The goose in Roz's arms," said Jaya to her brother, "that must be her son."

All of Roz's stories came flooding back to the children. The robot, the island, the wild animals, the adventures. Those stories seemed so fanciful. Could they really be true?

"You are correct, children, those robot stories are about me," admitted Roz, with a hint of sadness in her voice. "There were so many times that I wanted to tell you the truth about my past, but I was afraid the truth would frighten you." The robot motioned to the goose in her arms. "This is my son. His name is Brightbill."

Reader, there's another important quality that children possess. In addition to being sneaky and smart, they're also compassionate. Children care about others, and about the world, and as Jaya and Jad gazed at Roz and Brightbill, their little hearts were full of compassion.

"Please do not tell your father about me," said Roz. "To him, I am just a machine. If he learns the truth, he will send me back to the robot factory, where I will be destroyed. But you must do what you feel is right. My life is in your hands now."

The children looked at each other and smiled.

"Don't worry, Roz," said Jaya.

"Your secret is safe with us," said Jad.

CHAPTER 39
THE ALLIES

Jaya and Jad would do anything to have their own mother back. So they understood how happy Brightbill and Roz must have felt in that moment. But they also understood that this happy moment couldn't last forever. Brightbill couldn't live on the farm, and Roz couldn't be her true self around their father. Life seemed so unfair.

The children knew what needed to happen.

"Roz, you need to go home," said Jaya.

"You need to be with your family and your friends on your island," said Jad.

"I wish I could go home, but your father would never allow it," said Roz.

"Just run away!" said the girl. "I ran away once—it was easy! But then I started feeling hungry, so I came home and made myself a sandwich."

"Running away might be easy for you, but not for me," said Roz. "Your father can track my movements. If he sees me trying to escape, he will think I am defective, and he will send me away to be destroyed."

An uncomfortable question popped into Jaya's mind. "Roz, don't take this the wrong way," she began, "but is it possible that you *are* defective?"

"Don't say that, Jaya!" cried her brother.

"No, it is okay," said the robot. "I have asked myself that same question. I do not feel defective. I feel...different. Is being different the same as being defective?"

"I don't think so," said Jaya. "Or else we're all a little defective."

"You saved my life, and now I'm going to save yours," said Jad, with a look of determination in his eyes. "I know you can only access farming information, Roz. So let us handle the research. There has to be a way for you to safely escape. But we'll need time to figure out a plan."

The robot exchanged a few animal words with her son. And then she said to the children, "Brightbill must soon lead his flock back to their wintering grounds. However, he can return here in the spring."

The boy slowly nodded. "We should have you ready by then."

The girl looked concerned. "Roz, even if you safely escape from the farm, how will you get all the way home to your island?"

"Leave that to Brightbill and me," said the robot. "Together, we will find our way home. I have faith in the two of us. And I have faith in the two of you."

CHAPTER 40

THE INSTINCTS

The next few days were a blur. Roz rushed through her daily tasks so she could have more time with the flock. The geese talked about Chitchat the squirrel, and the Beaver family, and the other animals on the island. Roz talked about the robot factory and the Shareefs and life on the farm.

But the geese were always aware of
their instincts, calling them back to
the warm wintering grounds. And
when they awoke one morning to find
the countryside dusted with snow, they knew it
was time to go.

By some miracle Roz and Brightbill had been reunited,
and now they had to say good-bye all over again. The
flock stood in the pasture with Roz as the children and
the herd looked on. Brightbill fluttered up to his mother's
shoulder and wrapped his wings around her face.

"I'll return in the spring," said the goose. "And then
you and I are going to find our way home."

"Please be careful," said the robot. "I do not want to
lose you again."

"We'll keep your son out of trouble," squawked Loudwing with a smile.

The geese waved good-bye to Roz and their new farm
friends. Then Brightbill shook his tail feathers, beat his
wings, and led his flock into the sky.

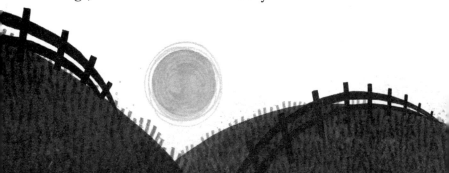

CHAPTER 41

THE WINTER

When Roz lived on the island, winter had seemed like one long, cruel blizzard. On Hilltop Farm winter wasn't quite so harsh. The temperature fell but then rose. Storms came and then went. Snow piled up and then melted away.

Roz spent winter preparing the farm for spring. She wanted everything to be perfect for when she left. She tuned up the machines, she made fertilizer from old grass clippings and manure, she planned which crops would be seeded in which fields. She carefully looked over the herd, making sure each cow was happy and healthy. She made long lists of supplies, and then Mr. Shareef placed big orders.

The Herding Machine hauled bales of hay into the pasture and the cows gathered around to eat, steam puffing from their mouths. Some of the cows were "dried off" and wouldn't be milked again until after the calving season. Others went to the milking parlor twice a day as usual. Bottles were filled, boxes were loaded, and the milk truck rolled away on its next delivery run. No matter the season, the dairy farm kept chugging along.

Every day after school, Jaya and Jad ran to their bedrooms and got right to their homework. And when their homework was finished, their secret studies began. They researched the design and construction and maintenance of ROZZUM robots, hoping to discover some way for Roz to safely escape. The information wasn't easy to find, but the children were persistent, and after weeks of work, they finally found what they were searching for.

CHAPTER 42

THE PLAN

Jaya pressed a button on the side of the milking parlor and the door hummed open. She and her brother stepped inside and wound their way past gleaming pipes and tanks and over to where Roz was cleaning some equipment.

"We found a diagram of your design!" said Jaya. "We think we can help you escape!"

"The problem is your Transmitter," said Jad. "That's the device that sends out your electronic signal. If we can remove your Transmitter, you'll be able to run away whenever you want, without anyone tracking you."

"Do you know how to remove it?" asked Roz.

"I think so." The boy chuckled nervously. "But we won't know for sure until we open you up and take a look."

"We'll have to do it late at night," said Jaya. "When Dad is sleeping."

"We just need to find a place where we can work in private," said Jad, rubbing his chin.

"How about the old barn?" said Roz. "It is quiet and hidden. I can prepare the barn today and you can operate on me tonight."

Everyone agreed, and the plan was set.

CHAPTER 43

THE OPERATION

Midnight, and the children were wide-awake in their beds. Jaya and Jad were waiting for their father to fall asleep. Once he was snoring deeply, they tiptoed past his bedroom, down the stairs, and out the back door.

They crept across the farm to a cluster of trees, and there was the old barn, looming above the undergrowth like a mountain. Its door was open a crack, and a wedge of light spilled outside. The children closed the door behind them, and walked past wooden railings and stairways and up a ramp to a platform in the back corner of the barn. Lanterns hung from the walls and cast their soft light upon a large table. Standing behind the table was the robot.

"Hello, children," said Roz. "How do you like our operating room?"

"It's a little dark," said Jaya. "But it'll work."

Jad pulled his computer from his pocket. As he brought up the diagram of Roz's body, his face tightened with worry. "We've never done anything like this before."

"Just do your best," said Roz, patting him on the back. "That is all I can ask of you."

The robot unfastened her tool belt and draped it over a railing. Then she lay flat on the table. It was time to begin.

Jaya looked down at Roz. "All set?"

Roz looked up at Jaya. "All set."

The girl felt under the robot's head, found the button with her fingers, and pressed it.

Click.

Roz's body relaxed.

Her quiet whirring slowly stopped.

Her eyes faded to black.

Jad took a deep breath. Then he grasped the robot's head in his hands and twisted until—*thwip*—it popped off. In the smooth socket where the head had just been was another button. Jaya pressed it and the robot's chest opened up. They peered into the hollow chest cavity and saw a tangle of tubes connected to a grid of boxes: these were the robot's electronic organs.

"That's the Transmitter," said Jad, pointing. The children reached into the robot's chest, carefully removed a box and a tube, and set them on the table.

"That was easy!" said Jaya, smiling.

"Actually, I think this is the Transmitter over here," said Jad, and he removed another box. Then Jaya removed another tube. The boy checked his computer and said, "I might have this backward." A bead of sweat rolled down his forehead as he removed another box.

"Wait, I think we should start over." Jaya nudged her brother out of the way and started plugging parts back into the robot's chest.

"You're doing it wrong." Jad nudged his sister out of the way and started removing parts again.

I don't know about you, reader, but I'm a little confused. So were the children. Pretty soon Roz's internal parts were strewn across the table, and nobody knew where anything was supposed to go.

"Why did you remove so many boxes?" yelled Jaya.

"Why did you remove so many tubes?" yelled Jad.

The siblings argued for a while.

Then they sat quietly for a while.

The children were tired and cranky and afraid that they'd never get Roz working again. Jaya slumped against the table and looked up at the ceiling. Then her eyes drifted to the lanterns dimly glowing above. And then she had an idea. She climbed onto a wooden railing, grabbed one of the lanterns from its hook, and climbed back down. When she held the lantern close to Roz's body, Jad noticed that there were different numbers lightly etched onto each of the internal parts. Now things were starting to make sense. The children quickly removed the correct box and tube, they put the robot back together, and they turned her on.

Click.

Roz's body tensed.

Her quiet whirring slowly started.

Her eyes began to glow.

But she didn't say a word.

"Are you okay?" said Jad.

Roz pointed to her mouth.

"Can you speak?" said Jaya.

Roz shook her head.

"She can't speak!" cried the boy. "We must have put something back in the wrong place!"

Click.

The children opened up Roz's body, rearranged some of her internal parts, and put her back together again.

Click.

Roz powered up and said, "Children, I can now speak, but I cannot move."

Click.

After hours of trial and error, and with morning light seeping into the barn, the operation was a success. Roz stood up, scanned her internal parts, and said, "Children, you did it! You removed my Transmitter! Thank you so much for your help."

"You're very welcome," said Jaya, yawning.

Jad checked his computer. "I can still see your signal on the map," he said. "Your Transmitter is still working, so keep it close until you leave the farm." And then he stuffed the little electronic device into the robot's tool belt.

"Children, there is a bit of bad news," said Roz in a serious tone. "I know you have been up all night long, but I am afraid it is time for you both to get ready for school."

CHAPTER 44

THE PATIENT ROBOT

After being trapped on Hilltop Farm for nearly a year, Roz was now free to run away anytime she liked. But without Brightbill to guide her, she wouldn't make it far. So the robot patiently waited for spring to come, and for her son to return, so they could begin their long journey home together.

CHAPTER 45

THE BARN CONVERSATIONS

As winter dragged on, Roz spent more of her time inside with the herd. There were long stretches of quiet. The cows chewed their hay. The robot tapped the farm computer. The wind gently rattled the windows. And then someone would start talking, someone else would chime in, and the quiet of the barn would gradually be overtaken by conversations like these.

"I am so bored." Tess was staring at the floor. "I can't wait until spring, when I can wander through tall grass and feel warm sunlight on my back. I just hope I don't die of boredom first!"

Old Annabelle snorted. "You young cows are spoiled rotten," she said. "Your lives are so easy, and still you find things to complain about!"

Tess rolled her eyes. "Yeah, yeah, we should be grateful for what we've got, you've told us before."

"Well, you *should* be grateful for what you've got!" said Annabelle. "I've lived on other farms, and trust me, you have nothing to complain about."

Tess couldn't help being curious, and she said, "What were those other farms like?"

"Oh, I'd rather not discuss them," said Annabelle in a low voice. "You see, I witnessed some terrible things on those farms. It was a blessing when I was moved here, but I often think about the animals I left behind. I hope they're okay."

The old cow sank into thought for a minute.

"I know life here isn't perfect," she said at last. "But we have so much to be grateful for. We have our lovely herd, and we have this beautiful barn, and—"

"And we have Roz," added Tess.

"And we have Roz." Annabelle turned and smiled at the robot in the corner. "Roz listens to us, and treats us with love and kindness, and she makes our lives as comfortable as she possibly can. We certainly will miss her when she's gone."

• • •

"Roz, why do humans need so much cow's milk?" said Lily as the other calves crowded around her. It was a question they'd all been wondering about.

"Well, there are billions of humans in the world," explained Roz, "and many of them drink milk and combine it with different ingredients to make different foods."

"What kinds of foods?" said another calf.

"Butter and cheese and yogurt are made with milk," said Roz. "Many desserts are also made with milk."

"What's a dessert?" said someone else.

"A dessert is a sweet food eaten at the end of a meal. Popular desserts include cake and custard and ice cream."

This answer only raised more questions.

"What is cake?"

"What is custard?"

"What is ice cream?"

Roz tried her best to explain these foods to the calves. But it wasn't easy. After all, the robot couldn't even perform the simple act of eating. How could she possibly describe the flavors and sensations of tasting delicious desserts?

Lily interrupted. "Just tell me this, Roz. When we're older, will our milk be used to make desserts?"

"Yes," said the robot.

The calves smiled. Then they trotted away, happy in the knowledge that, someday, they'd help to bring sweet and delicious things into the world.

"It is almost spring," said Roz to the herd. "It is almost time for me to run away, back home to the wilderness. I am sorry that I must leave, but you will all be well cared for when I am gone, I promise."

Cows began mooing from their stalls.

"Don't worry about us, Roz."

"There's no need to apologize."

"We understand why you're running away."

Lily poked her head through the railings of her stall and said, "I could never run away to the wilderness. I would be too frightened!"

"I'd love to roam through the wilderness!" said Tess. "It sounds so exciting!"

"No wilderness for me, thank you very much," said Annabelle. "I just want a quiet, cozy life."

"I have plenty to fear in the wilderness," said Roz. "However, I have more to fear here. I can never be my true self around humans. And so I must try to return to my home.

"I only wish I could do it by myself," she went on. "But I need help. I could never escape from the farm without the children, and I could never find my way home without my son. I feel bad for asking so much of them."

"Don't feel bad," said Lily. "Brightbill and the children want to help you. They love you! We all do. The farm won't feel the same without you, Roz. But we know you're doing the right thing."

The herd agreed with Lily. And throughout the barn, cows quietly nodded their heads.

CHAPTER 46

THE SPRING

With each passing day, the sun climbed a little higher and its rays grew a little warmer. The last patches of snow melted away and color returned to the land. The pasture, the fields, the trees, they all were turning bright green, and the air slowly filled with the fresh smells of spring.

Many of the cows had been steadily growing bigger, and now calving season had arrived. When the time was

right, each cow went out to the pasture so her calf could be born in soft grass. The robot stood nearby, just in case anyone needed her help, but nobody ever did. Even the first-time mothers knew what to do instinctively. And soon, newborn calves were frolicking around the farm.

Spring was a happy, exciting time, and yet Roz was distracted. More and more, she found herself looking to the skies, hoping to see Brightbill and his flock. She knew they were on their way.

CHAPTER 47

THE DINNER

Mr. Shareef hopped out of the truck with his arms full of shopping bags. He limped toward the farmhouse, dragging his leg in the usual way. And then he fell. Roz ran over and found the man sprawled on the driveway, groceries scattered around him.

"Are you okay?" she said, pulling him to his feet.

"I'm fine," he grumbled.

Roz started picking up the groceries and said, "Let me help you inside."

A minute later the two of them were stepping into the house. Jackets and hats hung from pegs on the wall. Shoes were lined up beneath a bench. The man peeled off his boots and hollered, "Kids, it's time to cook dinner!"

Footsteps pounded across the ceiling and the children came flying down the staircase with their dog.

"Is Roz having dinner with us?" said Jaya.

"Roz doesn't eat!" said Jad.

"I know that! But she could sit with us."

"How about it, Roz?" said Mr. Shareef. "Care to join us for dinner?"

The robot stared at the family.

The family smiled at the robot.

"What would you like me to do?" said Roz.

In a very proper voice, Jad said, "I would greatly enjoy the pleasure of your company for dinner."

In a very improper voice, Jaya said, "I order you to stay for dinner!"

The children didn't wait for a response. They snatched the groceries from Roz and scampered off. Oscar ran after them, barking, "Is that food? It smells like food! I want food!"

The wooden floor creaked as Roz followed Mr. Shareef through the living room. A comfy chair and a sofa faced a darkened electronic screen. Above the fireplace hung a painting of a familiar old barn. Doorways led to other rooms. Roz glanced into Mr. Shareef's office and saw a portrait of his family, including his wife. Mrs. Shareef was pretty, with dark, curly hair and a bright smile. It was the same smile Roz saw on the children.

"Look, Jaya's crying like a baby!" came Jad's giggly voice from the kitchen. When Roz walked in, the girl was chopping an onion with tears streaming down her cheeks.

"Roz, I order you to chop this onion for me," said Jaya, wiping her eyes.

The robot picked up a knife and in a flash the onion was perfectly chopped and dumped into a bowl. Clearly, Roz was designed to chop onions.

"Roz, I order you to take the night off!" Mr. Shareef laughed. "The kids and I want to cook. We enjoy it!"

More vegetables were chopped, skillets started sizzling, delicious aromas swirled together, and before long a magnificent meal was set on the dinner table. Oscar positioned himself below, to catch food scraps, and everyone else took a seat.

Mr. Shareef turned to his daughter. "Would you like to say grace?"

The girl lowered her head. "Thank you, God, for this yummy food we're about to gobble down, amen."

"Thank you, Jaya," said Mr. Shareef with a wink. "And thank you, Roz, for everything you've done this past year. I had my doubts, but now I can't imagine what we'd do without you."

The children looked at each other.

Then the family grabbed their knives and forks and dug into dinner. A colorful, leafy salad. A plate of sautéed asparagus. Creamy mashed potatoes and buttered bread and tall glasses of milk. The meal was beautiful. But as Roz scanned the table, her eyes kept returning to the roasted chicken. It was about the size of Brightbill. Suddenly, the robot was full of questions.

Do chickens live happy lives?

Did this chicken know it would be eaten?

Were humans bad for eating animals?

No, thought Roz, humans are simply following their instincts, like all creatures, like Roz herself. At least the Shareefs honored this animal by giving thanks, and by turning it into a beautiful, nourishing meal.

After he'd finished eating, Mr. Shareef stepped out of the room, and he returned a moment later carrying a violin and a bow. "Growing up, I dreamed of being a musician," he said, thumping back into his chair. He tuned the instrument, put it under his chin, and started to play.

His bow glided back and forth, his fingers danced across the strings, and a lovely old folk song filled the room. Mr. Shareef tapped his foot as the notes rang out, soft and then loud, slow and then fast. The song ended with a flourish, and the music faded to silence. Then he rested the violin on his knee. "This instrument has been in our family for a very long time," he said, "since the days when Cyrus Shareef first built the farm."

Cyrus Shareef.

Roz knew that name. She unsnapped a pocket on her tool belt and pulled out the small journal. "I discovered this in the old barn," she said, handing it over.

The children huddled around their father as he took the journal. They read their ancestor's name on the cover. Then they carefully opened it and turned the brittle pages. "I've never seen this journal before," said Mr. Shareef. "It's a piece of our family history. Kids, look at how they used to milk cows...."

Roz left the Shareefs like that, examining the journal, learning about their family's history. But what about their family's future? Their lives were difficult. They needed help. And Roz was about to run away forever. As she marched back to the barn that night, the robot felt something like worry and confusion and guilt.

CHAPTER 48

THE RETURN

The robot's feelings of worry and confusion and guilt went away as soon as she heard her son's voice echoing across the farm.

"Ma, we're back!"

Brightbill's flock appeared above the pasture, flapping and honking and laughing. They glided down to Roz, and Brightbill took his place on his mother's shoulder.

"I told you we'd keep your son out of trouble!" squawked Loudwing.

"Thank you, everyone!" The robot spoke in her most cheerful voice. "It is so good to see all of you again."

The cows trotted over, grinning and happily mooing to the geese. While the herd and the flock caught up with each other, Roz and Brightbill slipped away to speak privately.

"What's the plan, Ma?" said Brightbill.

"The plan is simple," said Roz. "Tonight, under the cover of darkness, I will run away from this farm. And then you and I will begin our journey home."

CHAPTER 49

THE GOOD-BYES

That evening was full of sad good-byes. The first good-bye was between the flock and their young leader. The other geese wanted to help Roz and Brightbill get home. But the journey would be dangerous, and Brightbill refused to put his flock at risk. He demanded they return to the island without him. The geese could feel their instincts urging them onward, and they knew Roz and Brightbill would look after each other, so they said their good-byes and took off into the night sky.

The next good-bye was between the robot and the cows. Roz marched into the pasture one last time as the herd gathered around.

"I guess this is it," said the robot. "Thank you all for being so kind to me."

Annabelle sniffled and said, "I really hate good-byes. But I'm glad you're going home where you belong. I just wish there was some way I could be helpful."

"Actually, there is something you can do." Roz unsnapped a pocket of her tool belt and took out the Transmitter. "You can hold on to this for me. Hopefully it will take a few days for Mr. Shareef to realize I am gone." Annabelle smiled as the robot gently tucked the small device under her collar.

Lily and the other calves suddenly swarmed around Roz and nuzzled her legs. They all had tears in their eyes. Tess wanted to lighten the mood, but she couldn't think of anything funny to say.

The other cows called out to their friend.

"We'll miss you, Roz!"

"Get home safely!"

"Don't forget about us!"

Roz waved to the herd. She said a silent good-bye to all the farm machines, parked in the shed. Then she followed the driveway out to the fields, with Brightbill on her shoulder and the children at her side.

The last good-bye was the hardest of all. Everyone was quiet as they walked through the silvery moonlight, past rows and rows of sprouting crops, and out to the farthest corner of the farthest field. Roz turned and faced Jaya and Jad. She looked past them, back to the distant lights of the farm buildings.

"I have prepared the farm for my departure," said Roz. "It will take care of itself for a while, but not forever."

"We can manage things, at least until we get another robot," said Jad. "This place won't be the same without you, but we'll be okay."

"What will you tell your father?" said Roz.

"That's for us to worry about," said Jaya. "You just worry about getting home."

Roz glanced down at the tool belt strapped across her chest. "Would you like this back?"

"No we would not!" said Jad.

"It was a gift just for you!" said Jaya.

The girl pulled her brother and her robot into a big, tight hug. Beneath the sounds of the crickets were the sounds of the children crying.

"How will we know you've made it home?" said Jad.

"We need to know how your story ends!" said Jaya.

The robot muttered some animal words to her son and then said to the children, "If a goose ever visits this farm

and presents you with a feather, you will know that I am home."

The children smiled through their tears and waited for their friends to leave. But the robot didn't move. More than anything, Roz wanted to go home. And yet she was conflicted. She cared about this family, and this farm, and now she was abandoning them. The robot lurched forward, then backward, again and again, as her computer brain struggled with all of these thoughts and feelings.

Finally, the children gave her the gentle push she needed. "Roz, we order you to run away."

And the robot did as she was told.

CHAPTER 50
THE FREE ROBOT

At long last, Roz was free! But as she ran away from Hilltop Farm, she didn't feel free. She felt something more like fear. She feared being seen and captured and destroyed. She feared for her son's safety. So Roz camouflaged herself, she avoided the fields and kept to the trees, and with Brightbill as her guide, she carefully crept north through farm country. The wild robot's long journey home had begun.

CHAPTER 51

THE AIRSHIP

The sun was up and our friends were on the move. They were traveling quickly and quietly along a narrow strip of forest that cut between vast crop fields. If not for that nagging fear of being spotted, it would have been a very pleasant hike.

Wind whispered through the leaves.

Insects hummed and chirped.

Farm machines rumbled in the distance.

And then there came a new sound. A buzzing sound. Our friends hid in the underbrush as an airship rose up from the horizon, ahead of them. It was a sleek white triangle, flying low and fast. Roz adjusted her vision and saw familiar robots gazing out the front window. RECO 1, RECO 2, and RECO 3 had been destroyed back on the island. Perhaps these robots were RECOs 4, 5, and 6?

"They're flying toward Hilltop Farm," said Brightbill.

"We need to keep moving," said Roz.

The airship disappeared to the south and the travelers continued north at a faster pace. They hurried through more strips of forest, passing squirrels and birds and groundhogs and other friendly creatures. But the robot and the goose had no time to chat.

Later that day, the trees came to an abrupt end. Roz and Brightbill stood at the forest edge and faced an ocean of wheat. The wheat was still young

and green. It gently waved in the wind, and spread out as far as they could see.

"What should we do?" asked Brightbill.

"We need to keep moving," said Roz, staring across the plains. "But I am not safe in the open. There must be more trees out there somewhere."

"I'll take a look," said Brightbill, and the goose launched himself skyward. Up, up, up he went, high into the air, until he finally stopped and floated, just a tiny winged shape against the blue, and then he dove back to his mother.

"There are trees in that direction," said Brightbill, pointing. "It's far, about thirty minutes at top speed."

"Then we had better get started," said Roz.

Our friends burst out from the underbrush, the robot sprinting through the field, the goose flying by her side. Roz had to concentrate to keep from slipping in the soft, muddy soil. But she stomped on, and far ahead, another line of trees slowly climbed into view.

Brightbill suddenly swooped up and out of sight as his mother kept running. Then he lowered back down beside her and squawked, "The airship is returning!"

Behind them, a tiny white triangle rose up from the

horizon. It was growing larger and louder by the second. If Roz was seen, her newfound freedom, and her life, would be over. She couldn't take any chances.

"Go on without me!" hollered the robot, and she dropped to the ground.

Brightbill hoped his mother knew what she was doing, and he flew on without her. Once he reached the trees he perched himself on a branch and looked back. His mother had vanished. The airship, however, seemed to fill the sky. Its shadow flitted across the ground where Roz had just been. But the ship didn't see her, and it detected no electronic signal, so it kept going, racing above the trees and over the next field. Its engine noise gradually faded, and it disappeared to the north.

"You can come out, Ma!" squawked Brightbill from his branch.

A column of wheat stood up in the field. The robot had rushed her camouflage, and it crumbled off her body when she started to march. As she approached the trees, Roz looked at Brightbill in the branches and said, "We need to keep moving."

CHAPTER 52

THE SCOUT

Would the airship return? Were the RECOs hunting for Roz? Was it only a matter of time before she was caught? It was impossible to know. So our friends tried not to worry about those troubling questions, and they continued sneaking through farm country, from one wooded area to the next.

Roz wore a disguise of mud and weeds and bark. At the first hint of trouble she would freeze—and instantly become a rotten old tree trunk. Then she'd wait for Brightbill to tell her that it was safe to move on. If there were humans or robots nearby, she might have to wait for hours.

Back on the island, Brightbill had practiced flying like hawks and owls and sparrows and vultures. He couldn't fly exactly like those other birds, of course, but he was

an expert at diving and swooping and darting and soaring. Now he used those skills to secretly scout out the countryside for his mother. He'd fly up from her shoulder and return a short time later to share his findings.

"We're coming to another farmhouse. Let's avoid it by cutting across this field."

"Beyond these trees is a highway. Stay here and I'll tell you when it's safe to cross."

"Straight ahead is a small town. But I can lead you around it."

Brightbill's advice was always good, and Roz always followed it, and together the travelers safely made their way through farm country.

CHAPTER 53

THE FARM COUNTRY

During their travels, our friends passed every kind of farm imaginable. Some farms grew crops in vast fields and orchards. Others grew crops in great glimmering greenhouses. Some farms let their animals graze through open pastures. Others kept their animals confined to small enclosures. Some farms had old-fashioned barns and sheds. Others had modern laboratories that made meat, eggs, and milk without any animals at all. There seemed to be an infinite number of ways to produce food for humans.

The farms were teeming with robot workers, and Roz couldn't resist spying on them as she carefully slunk past. The robots worked the fields and machines and livestock, their bodies shining in the sun, shimmering in the heat. This must have been how Roz looked, back on Hilltop Farm. Were any of these robots like her? Were any of them quietly dreaming of escape? Or were they all just mindless machines, content with their place in the world?

CHAPTER 54

THE MOUNTAINS

The flat plains of farm country gradually rolled into hills and valleys. There were fewer crop fields and more forests. The hills grew taller, the valleys sank deeper, the farms disappeared entirely. Our friends had reached the mountains.

Brightbill floated on the wind as Roz climbed the slopes. They passed craggy rock formations and rushing waterfalls and meadows lush with flowers. The robot could have hiked on and on, never slowing or stopping, but the goose needed to rest.

As the stars came out each evening, they found a safe location to settle down. Frost was common in the higher regions, and Roz took the lighter from her tool belt and built small campfires to keep her son warm. They sat around the crackling flames, reminiscing about life on the island, until Brightbill drifted off to sleep. As the sun came up each morning, they'd clear away all traces of their campsite and set off again, deeper into the mountains.

Eagles perched on jagged cliffs.

Fish splashed through gurgling streams.

Chipmunks bickered in the thick undergrowth.

It felt good to be back in wilderness. But this place wasn't home. So the travelers kept a brisk pace. The robot adjusted her camouflage to match her surroundings. In the forest, she wore leaves and tree bark. In the meadows, she wore grass and wildflowers. In the rocky terrain, she wore dirt and weeds. Even way out there in the wilderness, she wanted to go unseen. What Roz didn't realize was that she was already being watched.

CHAPTER 55

THE ATTACK

Wide mountain meadows made the robot nervous. While hiking through them, she felt exposed and easy to spot. Camouflage helped, but it was hard not to notice a walking clump of wildflowers. Especially one accompanied by a goose. And it was in one of those wide meadows that trouble caught up with our friends.

From the corner of her eye, Roz sensed movement. She turned but saw only tall grass blowing in the breeze. Then a twig snapped, but the sound was swallowed by a distant roll of thunder. It wasn't until the wind changed and a musky scent wafted by that the robot understood the danger.

"I smell wolves," whispered Roz.

Brightbill's eyes grew big and round, and he whispered back, "What should we do?"

Before Roz could reply, two wolves leaped out from the brush. They charged toward the robot, snarling and snapping their jaws. Roz heaved her son toward the sky so that he could fly to safety, and then she burst into a sprint. The robot zigged and zagged across the meadow, trying to shake off the wolves. But when she dashed through a patch of soft ground, she slipped and toppled into the grass.

The wolves quickly surrounded their prey, heads low, ears drawn back, deep growls rumbling through their teeth.

"Remember us, Roz?" said the huge male with the scar.

"Hello again, Shadow," said the robot, slowly getting to her feet. "And I believe your name is Barb."

"You have a good memory," said the female wolf.

"Actually, I have a perfect memory," said the robot.

"And yet you've forgotten your rifle." A toothy smile appeared on Shadow's face. "You aren't so tough without your rifle, are you?"

Barb sniffed the breeze. "Where's your pet goose?" And then she saw Brightbill perched in a lone tree in the middle of the meadow.

"He is not my pet," said Roz. "He is my son."

Shadow chuckled. "We've heard the stories about

the robot mother and her son, the goose. They're very touching." He turned and barked, "Join us, Brightbill! We'd love to meet you up close!"

"Stay where you are, son!" hollered Roz. "I will take care of them!"

"You'll take care of *us*?" growled Shadow. "No, Barb and I will take care of *you*."

The robot's computer brain hummed as it tried to make a plan. The wolves were stalking toward her—any second now they would attack! Roz had to do something, anything, so she stalled.

"Shadow, Barb, is it just the two of you?" Roz scanned the meadow and saw no other wolves. "Where is the rest of your pack?"

Well, that was the wrong question to ask, because the fur on Shadow's back stood up and he snarled, "*This is my pack now!*" Then the wolves pounced.

But Roz wasn't there. With all the strength in her legs, the robot launched herself up and away, and now she was soaring through the air in a long, graceful arc. Once her feet stomped back to the ground, she launched

herself up and away again. With giant, arcing strides, the robot bounded across the meadow in the direction of her son.

At first, the wolves were baffled by the robot's strange escape. But they were expert hunters. They raced after her, studying her closely, watching where she landed. And when Roz made her final leap toward Brightbill's tree, a heavy paw knocked her off balance. She tumbled through the air and slammed against the trunk. Leaves shook loose, dead branches crashed down, but the robot held tight to the tree.

"Are you okay, Ma?" said the goose as he fluttered to his mother's side.

"Just some light scrapes," said the robot, and she pulled herself onto a sturdy branch.

Below the tree, the wolves were howling with laughter. "Nice try, Roz!" said Shadow. "But you can't outrun us. Wolves are built for chasing!"

"You are wasting your time," said the robot. "You cannot eat me, and you will never catch my son."

"You still don't get it, Roz," growled the wolf. "I'm not hunting you for food. I'm hunting you for revenge."

CHAPTER 56

THE TORCH

Our friends were stuck in that tree. They sat in the upper branches, high above the wolves, trying to calculate an escape. Brightbill could fly off whenever he liked, but Roz had to come down eventually. And when she did, the wolves would be ready.

Shadow and Barb stretched out in the shade. They glanced around and licked their fur and sniffed the mountain air. The wolves looked comfortable, and yet there was tension between them.

"I'm hungry," growled Barb. "I want to eat rabbits and deer, or maybe go back to farm country and prey on livestock. Anything is better than hunting a creature that can't be eaten."

"You can eat all the animals you like," said Shadow, "after we kill the robot."

Barb grumbled with frustration. She didn't understand Shadow's need for revenge. But for now, she stayed loyal to her mate.

Day turned to night, and the wolves started yawning. Barb's eyelids became heavy. Shadow's body became weary. Then the soothing song of the crickets lulled them both to sleep.

The sight of sleeping wolves reminded Roz of those long winter nights on the island, when wild animals crawled into her warm home and slept. She remembered the frightened look in their eyes as they saw fire for the first time. And this gave Roz an idea.

Quietly, she broke off a dead branch from the tree trunk. Then she took the lighter from her tool belt and held a flame under the branch's knobby end until it was blazing. And then she

dropped

down

to the ground.

Shadow and Barb snapped awake to find the world bathed in orange light. Towering above them, looking like a demon, was the robot. Her eyes were glowing. Her mouth was roaring. In her hand was a torch, flames rippling, embers whirling into the air.

The wolves had never seen fire. It was beautiful, and it was terrible. Deep inside, they felt their wolf instincts telling them this ball of swirling light was dangerous. Their instincts told them to run for their lives, and when Roz lunged toward them, they ran. Barb yelped, Shadow whimpered, and the two wolves raced away from the fire just as fast as they could.

CHAPTER 57

THE STONES

At first light, Roz nudged Brightbill awake, and the travelers continued north through the mountains. The goose stood on his mother's shoulder as she marched. His eyes darted around nervously, searching for any sign of the wolves. But the wolves were gone. And our friends turned their attention to a new problem.

The weather out there was always changing. Roz and Brightbill had seen many calm, sunny days suddenly turn to wind or fog or sleet, or even snow. Our friends expected bad weather, so they hardly noticed when heavy rain came sweeping down a valley. But there was something odd about this rain.

Brightbill squinted at the oncoming storm and said, "Ma, why is the rain bouncing off the ground?"

Bouncing rain? That didn't seem right. The robot's computer brain went to work and she found the correct word. "That is not rain," she said. "That is hail."

CLANG! A hailstone bounced off Roz's chest. Another one swooshed into the weeds. Then the sky opened up and hailstones were everywhere. They tore through leaves and branches. They ricocheted off rocks and roots. They flattened flowers and bushes.

To the robot, the hailstones were annoying. To the goose, they were deadly. A stone hit Brightbill's shoulder and he fell to the ground. Roz scooped him up, hunching over, protecting him from the falling stones, but the hailstorm might kill the poor bird if they couldn't find cover soon.

Frantically, the robot scanned the area for any type of shelter. And there it was. On the far side of the valley, beside a winding river, was a cabin. It was old and shabby, but it had a roof, and that's what our friends needed most.

Roz held her son close, pumped her legs, and thundered across the valley. Heavy hailstones hissed into the grass and squelched into the mud and clanged off our robot. There was a soft thump, and Brightbill cried out in pain. Roz bounded over the rushing river in a single leap, landed without breaking stride, and kept running. Now she could hear hailstones cracking against the cabin, louder and louder. The robot stomped up to the front door, turned the handle, and stepped inside.

CHAPTER 58
THE CABIN

The hailstorm was brief but violent. Its icy stones were quickly melting away, but the damage would linger on. The valley was littered with shredded leaves and wildflowers. Wounded animals were hobbling back to their homes. Several unlucky birds lay limp in the grass.

Inside the cabin, Roz was standing by the window. She held Brightbill in her arms, his bruised body wrapped in an old blanket. The robot knew everything there was to know about caring for animals. But all her son needed was time. His injuries would heal on their own.

"Go on without me, Ma," said the goose in a weak voice. "I'll catch up to you when I'm feeling better."

"That is ridiculous," said the robot. "What kind of mother would leave her injured son behind?"

"But, Ma—"

"Stop talking," interrupted Roz. "You need to rest."

Brightbill tried to argue, but he was already falling asleep.

The cabin was simple, just a square room with a wood stove, two chairs beside a table, and a couple of cots rotting in the corner. Dusty mugs and bowls sat on a shelf; otherwise the walls were bare. It was clear no humans had been there for a very long time. However, it seemed that some other creature had moved in. The whole place had a foul odor. Lumps of feces were strewn about, and little footprints trailed away from a dark hole in the floor.

Roz leaned over the hole, and in the language of the animals, she said, "Hello? Is anyone down there?"

Something moved, and then a pair of shining eyes looked up from the darkness. "Who are you?" said a voice. "I didn't invite you into my home!"

"I am sorry to intrude," said the robot. "My son and I were only trying to escape the hailstorm."

"Your son?" said the voice. "Is that him in your arms? Let me see."

Very gently, the robot lifted a fold of cloth and revealed the sleeping goose.

"He must take after his father," said the voice.

"He is my adopted son," the robot explained. "My name is Roz, and this is Brightbill."

The shining eyes blinked, and the voice squeaked with excitement.

"You're Roz and Brightbill? The birds have been singing about you for months! You're living legends!"

"Technically, I am not living," said the robot.

"You seem pretty alive to me," said the voice. "Either way, it's nice to meet you. They call me Sprinkles." With that, the creature crawled up through the hole in the floor. She was covered in black fur from her nose all the way to the tip of her fluffy tail. Well, except for those white stripes running down her back. You see, Sprinkles was a skunk. The robot took one look at her and stepped backward.

Sprinkles frowned. "You know, Roz, skunks only get stinky when we're nervous."

"Are you nervous now?"

"Well, sort of, but in a good way! I'm honored to meet you! Please, pull up a seat and tell me what brings you here."

Sprinkles hopped onto the table and listened as Roz described their journey. The skunk was a very good listener. While Roz spoke, Sprinkles nodded politely and said things like "Oh my" and "Is that right?" and "You don't say!"

This went on until Brightbill began to stir. "Ma, I'm thirsty," he whispered.

"There's a creek right out back," said Sprinkles. "And those might be useful." She motioned to the bowls on the shelf. "Please, help yourself to anything. My home is your home."

It turns out skunks can be quite hospitable. Sprinkles invited the visitors to stay as long as they liked, and so our friends spent Brightbill's recovery in the cabin. The goose mostly slept. The robot brought him water and food. The skunk made sure they both were comfortable.

A few mornings later, sunlight streamed in through the window and onto Brightbill. He was squawking and waddling and fluttering through the cabin. His injuries had healed and he was eager to continue their journey.

"Thank you for everything, Sprinkles!" The robot waved as she marched away from the cabin with her son on her shoulder.

"Glad I could help!" called the skunk. "Misunderstood creatures like us gotta look out for each other!"

CHAPTER 59

THE STRANGE WILDERNESS

Another gloomy day had settled over the mountains. Here and there, the sun broke through the clouds and bright streaks came shining down like spotlights. One of those bright streaks swept over a rugged mountainside and found our friends. For a moment, the robot and the goose basked in warm sunlight. Then the patch of light moved on and rolled into the next valley, where it sparkled across a strange industrial site.

A patchwork of large, boxy structures was nestled among the trees. Broken walkways clung to the walls. Ramps and pipes slanted up from holes in the ground. The robot's computer brain identified the site. It was a deserted coal mine.

This was a strange kind of wilderness. Scattered throughout that mountain range were ghosts of human activity. Overgrown railways. Rusted automobiles. Spindly towers perched on mountaintops. Faded signs with messages like *No Trespassing* and *No Hunting*. It seemed humans had once lived and worked in this wilderness, only to leave it all behind.

In places, though, there was still activity. Robot activity. Armies of robot workers methodically dug new tunnels and built new dams and worked in new mining operations. They took down abandoned buildings and hauled away truckloads of litter. Our friends were curious about these working robots, but they kept a safe distance, and went on their way.

CHAPTER 60
THE HUNTERS

Crack!

A gunshot echoed through the mountains. There weren't many hunters willing to trek into that wilderness, but those who did were serious. They camped out, wore camouflage, and fired traditional rifles for the sport of it.

Crack!

Roz and Brightbill were desperate to stay clear of the hunters. However, that was proving difficult. The trees were tightly packed together and the undergrowth was tough and tangled. So they followed the deer paths that cut through this part of the forest. But they never knew when or where the next shot would be fired.

Crack!

The gunshots were growing louder. Our friends

slowed to a crawl, afraid of being seen or heard. And then the chatter of forest animals fell silent.

CRACK!

A bullet whizzed through the undergrowth and a deer went bounding away. At the same time, birds screeched and flapped into the air. Unfortunately, one of those birds was Brightbill. Scared and confused, the young goose fluttered up to a tree limb just as two hunters emerged from the bushes.

"What's a goose doing alone in these mountains?" said Hank, staring up at Brightbill. "And what's it doing in a tree?"

"There must be something wrong with it," said Miguel. "Maybe you should put it out of its misery."

Hank reloaded his rifle. "We're here to hunt deer," he said, "but it looks like we're having goose for dinner."

Had the hunters known Brightbill the way we do, reader, I'm sure they would have left him alone. But they knew nothing about him. To them, Brightbill was just another goose, a meal, and they were getting hungry.

The hunter raised his rifle.

He took a deep breath.

His finger reached for the trigger.

And then a fierce gust of wind suddenly blew across

the forest floor. No, not wind. Footsteps! Something was stomping toward the hunters! Their rifles were ripped away, bent into hooks, and thrown aside.

The men had hunted all manner of beasts, but they'd never come across this…this…well, they didn't know what this thing was. It looked like a tree stump, standing on two long roots, with branches hanging from its sides. The men stumbled backward, eyes and mouths opened wide. Then they turned and ran, and their terrified noises trailed off through the leaf litter.

The goose was terrified too. He slumped off his branch and into his mother's arms. The poor bird was trembling with fear, but he was unharmed.

"I am so sorry, Brightbill," said the robot. "I should have acted sooner. You are safe now, I promise."

CHAPTER 61
THE GUIDE

A light drizzle was falling on the travelers. Although they weren't actually traveling at the moment. They were standing still and staring up at a steep mountain of rocks. The robot had plenty of rock-climbing experience, but one bad fall out there and she could be stranded forever. So Roz carefully picked her way up the slippery slope, while Brightbill fluttered along beside her.

They hadn't gone far when there came the sound of hooves clattering on stone, and then a horned creature leaped from the mist and smashed right into the robot.

CLANG!—Roz went flying backward.

CLANG!—Roz crashed onto the ground.

Standing on the rocks above the robot was a wild ram. He had big, curling horns and a crazed look in his eyes.

Brightbill flew to his mother's side, ready to defend her. "Stay away from my mama!" he hissed, spreading his wings.

But rather than charging, the ram hung his head and started to cry. "Oh, I'm so sorry!" he blubbered. "I don't want to hurt anyone. Sometimes I just lose control and smash things. I feel awful about it, really I do!"

Roz brushed herself off. "I believe those are your instincts," she said. "We all have them—they can be very powerful. I only hope your instincts do not end up breaking me."

"Don't worry," the ram sniffled. "I'll try not to let my instincts break you."

"I appreciate that," said the robot.

"My name's Thud," said the ram. "Which way are you headed?"

"We are trying to find our way out of these mountains," said Roz. "But they never seem to end."

"You're almost there!" said Thud. "Let me show you the way—it's the least I can do after smashing you."

The ram pranced away and led our friends to a narrow path that wound up the rocky mountainside. Roz tried to stay close, but Thud was born to climb. He easily scrambled up the steep slopes and vanished into the mist. A minute later his friendly voice called out, "For a creature without hooves, you're not a bad climber!" And there he was, peering down from a cliff ledge.

The path opened into a foggy meadow where a whole flock of wild sheep were grazing. They reminded Roz of the cows, grazing in the pasture, and she wondered how Hilltop Farm was doing without her.

Thud pranced through the flock. "These are my new friends," he announced without stopping. "They're lost, so I'm guiding them out of the mountains." The sheep raised their heads. Thud had a habit of making weird friends, but these two were definitely the weirdest. The flock watched as the ram, the robot, and the goose continued up the mountain and disappeared into the mist.

Higher and higher they climbed, above the tree line, to where there were only rocks and scrubby plants and trickling mountain streams. They occasionally came upon a dirt road or a hiking trail, and the ram trotted across casually, while our friends crept across cautiously.

At one point, the ram got that crazed look in his eyes again. His horns came flying at the robot and she jumped out of the way just in time. Then Thud cried and apologized for his instincts, Roz forgave him, and the group carried on.

They finally hiked up from the mist and onto a mountain ridge. Above, the sky was clear. Below, a blanket of puffy clouds spread outward in every direction. The sun was setting, and the western clouds were burning pink.

Roz thought of the mountaintop on her island. If only she could be watching the sunset from that peak instead of this one. But they still had a long, long way to go.

Thud pointed our friends to one last path. "This will take you down from the mountains and through the foothills," he said, smiling.

The ram suddenly got that crazed look in his eyes again, and the robot prepared to jump. But this time Thud pulled himself together. He said good-bye to the travelers, and then he pranced away.

CHAPTER 62

THE SHOWDOWN

Daybreak in the foothills, and thick gray fog was everywhere. With such poor visibility, the travelers relied on their other senses. They smelled salty air. They felt sandy soil. They heard seagulls screeching and waves breaking. And then they heard the long, low note of a ship's horn. *Hmmmmmmm.* Somewhere in the distance, hidden by the fog, was the ocean.

As if to answer the ship, there came another long, low note. But it wasn't a horn, it was a howl. A wolf was following our friends.

Brightbill beat his wings and squawked, "Mama, run!"

Roz ran downhill, deeper into the gloom. Her feet stomped the sandy soil, leaving behind a trail of footprints. There was no time to hide her tracks, so she just kept running. Blurry shapes faded in and out of the fog, and her eyes darted around to see if they were rocks or bushes or wolves. But the robot should have watched where she was going. She slipped and thumped into the sand, and before she could get up, Shadow was on top of her.

The wolf was heavy and strong. He pinned Roz to the ground and locked his teeth onto her tool belt. At last, he had caught his prey! Violently, wildly, he thrashed the robot from side to side. Roz tried to squirm free, but Shadow's grip was tight. There was only one thing to do. She reached down beside the wolf's snarling jaws and fumbled with the buckle, and suddenly she was loose. Shadow staggered backward, the belt dangling from his mouth, as Roz stomped away.

Brightbill had been circling overhead this whole time and now he squawked desperate warnings to his mother.

"Look out for those rocks!"
"Shadow is gaining on you!"
"There are buildings ahead!"

Roz burst through a row of hedges and onto the main street of a seaside village. It was still early, and it was still foggy, and Roz was halfway through the village before anyone saw her. A man had just left for his morning walk when the robot and the wolf came galloping down the street. The man decided his walk could wait, and he hurried back inside.

Shadow swiped at Roz's heels, but the robot leaped away. She soared over a house and landed on the other side. The wolf dashed around the yard, only to see her leaping away once more.

This time Roz landed in shallow water. Waves gently sloshed against her ankles. The robot backed into the ocean, up to her waist, and then automatically stopped. Her Survival Instincts wouldn't let her go any farther.

"There's nowhere left to run," Shadow growled as he prowled onto the beach. "Either fight or swim."

Roz was trapped. Her body lurched forward and backward as her computer brain struggled to find an escape. And then Brightbill came to her rescue.

"This way, Mama!"

Roz didn't hesitate. She launched herself up from the shallows, toward her son's voice. Salt water streamed off her body as she soared through the air. Then her feet pounded into the sand beside Brightbill, who was perched atop an old rowboat.

By the time Shadow arrived, our friends were rowing away from shore. The wolf's face twisted with rage, and he howled from the water's edge. "You made a fool of me, Roz! My pack and my mate have left me! Now I'm just a worthless lone wolf! All because of you!"

Roz felt sorry for Shadow. She never meant for any of this to happen. But she had her own troubles. The robot's greatest fear was deep water, and now she was paddling through the waves and out to sea.

CHAPTER 63
THE ROWBOAT

The sun was shining, the fog was thinning, the robot was rowing. Roz was no thief, and she didn't like taking that old rowboat. But judging from its appearance, it had been abandoned years ago. She hoped it wouldn't be missed.

Anybody who's rowed one of these boats knows you're supposed to face backward. That can make it tough to see where you're going. This wasn't a problem for Roz, however. She started off rowing normally, and after several strokes of the oars, her head spun around until she was facing forward. And what she saw was blue sky, and dark waves, and a sliver of green on the horizon.

"We're in a bay," said Brightbill, swooping down into the boat. "To the north is that distant coastline. To the east is open water. To the west is a seaport. And to the south is the village, and the wolf."

It seemed the travelers had no choice but to cross the bay. Luckily, Roz could row long and fast. Brightbill settled in for the ride, and the robot's mechanical muscles started pumping. She pulled and pulled and pulled on the oars, and the rowboat glided through the waves.

Roz was nervous. Time and again, the robot's Survival Instincts had stopped her from going into deep water. Now an old rowboat was all that separated her from the murky depths. She couldn't wait to feel solid ground beneath her feet again.

As they rowed deeper into the bay, the waves got larger and rougher. Gigantic swells of water rolled in from the open ocean and started tossing the boat around like a toy. The waves finally became too much for Brightbill. He spread his wings, lifted up on the breeze, and anxiously looked at the choppy surf ahead.

"Row faster!" he squawked. "I don't know how much more the boat can take!"

Roz tried to power through. She rowed faster and faster, until the boat was skimming across the water. Too fast. The left oar snapped, then the right, and suddenly the boat was at the mercy of the waves.

"Hold on, Mama!" cried the goose. "Here comes a big one!"

The rowboat was pulled up the side of a towering wall of water. It teetered at the top. And then the boat went crashing down the other side with such force that the whole thing splintered apart! Roz felt water surging up around her. She clung to debris and kicked her legs, but she wouldn't stay afloat for long.

The robot began to sink.

The goose floated above.

The ocean rolled and sloshed.

Then there was a sudden burst of air from somewhere nearby. Brightbill looked toward the noise but saw only sea spray drifting on the breeze. And when he looked back to his mother, she was dipping below the surface.

"What can I do, Mama?" Brightbill cried from the air. "Tell me what to do!"

"There is nothing more you can do!" came Roz's gargling voice. "I am sorry!"

The young goose could only watch as the ocean dragged the robot

down

down

down.

CHAPTER 64
THE SEA CREATURE

Brightbill hovered on the wind and watched his poor mother sinking into the depths. He could still see her body sparkling brightly against the darkness. But she was fading fast.

The goose closed his eyes, hoping this was all a bad dream. He heard the distant horns of ships by the seaport. He heard buoys clanging in the harbor. He heard ocean waves churning and frothing, louder and louder. And louder. And LOUDER!

The goose opened his eyes and saw the ocean bulging upward. A giant sea creature was rising from the deep! It breached the surface and sent waves rolling away. The creature had a large mouth and long fins and a wide back that curved down into the water. There was a loud burst, and mist shot up from a blowhole. As you might have guessed, reader, that giant creature was a whale.

More of the whale emerged from the darkness until something sparkled in the sunlight. It was Roz! She was sprawled across the whale's back, wet, limp, and life-less.

CHAPTER 65

THE WHALE

The whale swam along the surface of the ocean, keeping our robot safely above the water, gently moving her away from the rough waves. Brightbill couldn't believe what he was seeing. Once the shock wore off, he fluttered down to the whale's back and leaned over his mother. There was no life in her eyes or her body. So the goose did the only thing he could think of.

Click.

Roz's eyes began to glow.

She uttered some human noises.

And then, in the language of the animals, the robot said, "Oh, Brightbill, am I happy to see you!"

The goose squawked with joy and hugged his mother's face, but she didn't move. She couldn't move. The robot had lost the use of her limbs. There were a few tense minutes and a few nervous glances. But as the sun beat down and the wind rushed over her, Roz felt her body drying out. Slowly, gradually, power returned to her arms, then her legs, and then she sat up and hugged her son.

Brightbill breathed a sigh of relief. "Mama, when you disappeared below the water, I thought you were gone forever."

"So did I," said Roz. "As I sank deeper and deeper, the ocean squeezed my body tighter and tighter. I lost control of my legs and my arms. The last thing I remember was a huge shape swimming toward me, and then I automatically shut down."

"That huge shape was a whale!" squawked the goose. "We're riding on her back right now!"

A low moan rumbled up through the whale's body. She splashed the water with her fins, and took long, wheezing breaths, and sprayed mist high into the air. Roz paid close attention to the whale's behavior and understood what she was saying.

The whale's name was Coral, and she was thrilled to meet our friends. She explained that a flock of geese had flown over the bay and regaled the coastal birds with the amazing story of the wild robot and her son, the goose.

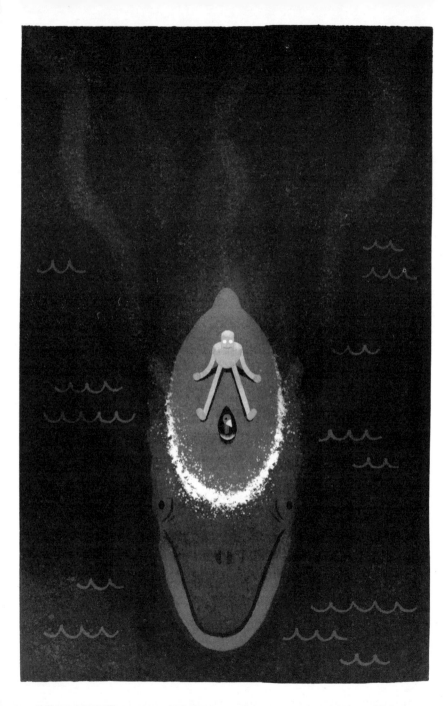

The coastal birds shared the story with the fish and the dolphins and anyone who would listen. In time, the story spread to every creature in the bay. When Coral saw the robot rowing and the goose flying overhead, she knew it had to be Roz and Brightbill. So she swam behind them, in case she could be helpful, and it was a good thing she did.

As Coral ferried our friends across the bay, the waves grew smaller and the coastline grew larger. Houses poked out from the trees. Sunbathers relaxed on the rocks. Boats motored away from the piers.

With so many humans around, Roz had to be careful. She lay flat against Coral's back while Brightbill flew ahead and scouted out the coastline. The goose directed the whale to a quiet, empty cove and soon the robot was standing on dry land again. Roz asked if there was some way she could repay Coral for saving her life, but the whale was just happy to help. She winked one of her enormous eyes, and then she sank beneath the waves.

Our friends marched inland, feeling lucky and grateful. But as they thought of the journey still to come, their good feelings gradually turned gloomy. Roz had nearly died crossing that bay. At some point, to get back to the island, she would have to cross an entire ocean.

CHAPTER 66

THE NEW LAND

Zoooooom!

Vrooooom!

Shooooom!

Automobiles were gliding up and down the road, passing fields and forests and clusters of houses. None of the passengers had any idea that a robot and a goose were watching from the weeds. Our friends had been hiding there for some time, waiting for the traffic to clear. But the automobiles kept coming. Roz noticed a drainage pipe that crossed under the road. The pipe was dark and grimy, but the travelers were getting desperate.

Moving through this new land was difficult. There were more humans and robots and buildings and roads than ever before. Roz and Brightbill traveled far out of their way, in wide circles, just to avoid small towns.

As the days passed, the scenery looked more familiar to Brightbill. He remembered flying over these lands on his first migration. He knew the towns would only get larger, and closer together, the farther they went. It would be much faster to sneak through the towns than to continue going around them. So, as night fell, Roz put on fresh camouflage, and with her son watching from the sky, she crept into a town.

CHAPTER 67

THE TOWN

Pookie was a big little dog. Her body was round, her legs were short, her ears were long. Although the dog looked funny, she was serious about protecting her home. She slapped her front paws on the windowsill and stared into the night to make sure all was well outside. But all was not well. A new clump of weeds had mysteriously sprouted in the yard. Pookie needed to take a closer look.

The dog whined by the back door until someone let her out. Then she scurried across the porch, down the steps, and over to the mysterious weeds. As Pookie approached, a raspy growl sounded in her throat.

"Where did these weeds come from?" she said to herself, sniffing. "They weren't here this afternoon!"

The weeds rustled in the breeze. And that was enough to set Pookie off. The dog barked and barked and barked, and then, astonishingly, the weeds spoke to her in a clear, calm voice.

"I am sorry if I disturbed you," said the weeds.

Pookie stopped barking.

"I was hoping to pass through without being seen," said the weeds. "But *you* saw me. You are a very good guard dog."

Pookie resumed barking.

"No, no, no! Shhhhhh!" said the weeds. "Please stop barking!"

But there was no stopping Pookie.

The clump of weeds decided to move. Like some sort of monster, the weeds rose up on two legs and leaped over the fence, into the neighboring yard. Felix had heard Pookie barking next door, and when the weedy monster landed in his yard, he started barking as well. So the monster kept going, leaping fences, from one yard to the next. Every house in the neighborhood seemed to have a dog, and they all began barking about the weedy monster. Reader, you and I know the monster was actually our robot in disguise. But the dogs never did figure out what happened that night.

Roz finally slunk into the shadows behind a school building and listened as the chorus of dogs settled down.

"That didn't go very well," said the goose as he landed beside his mother.

"No, it did not," said the robot.

"This will only be tougher in daylight."

"I know. I will have to try something else."

Early the next morning, the sun started rising, automobiles started driving, robots started running errands. However, one of those robots was not like the rest. Roz had picked every speck of dirt from her body, and now she blended in with all the normal robots going about their normal morning routines. Our robot was hiding in plain sight.

Roz marched through town, turning left and right down the streets, as Brightbill watched from above. Along the way, she passed a wide variety of robots all going about their business. There was even another ROZZUM robot marching around, who looked identical to our Roz, except she was shinier and had a different unit number. It occurred to ROZZUM unit 7134 that if anyone noticed her unit number, it might bring a swift response from the RECOs. But as she continued past houses and shops and humans and robots, there didn't seem to be any danger. Everything was going smoothly, until she heard an airship flying toward the town.

Our robot felt something like dread as she waited for a sleek white ship to appear. If the RECOs found her now, there would be no escape. But the ship that appeared wasn't white, it was black, and it flew over without stopping. Roz was safe, and suddenly she was dreaming about airships.

Returning to the island would be so easy with a ship. She and Brightbill would climb in, fire up the engines, and be home in no time at all. But it was an impossible dream. There was no safe way for our robot to get an airship. She had to find some other way home. First she had to find her way out of this town. So Roz focused on her surroundings and continued marching along the sidewalks, just like a normal robot.

CHAPTER 68

THE STATION

At the edge of town, where the houses stopped and the countryside began, was a small train station. Two platforms sat on either side of the tracks. Humans and robots were standing around, waiting for the next train to arrive. Nobody paid any attention to our robot as she calmly marched past. When Roz was safely out of sight, she slipped into the woods where Brightbill was hiding.

The goose opened his mouth to speak, but the station bells started ringing. Speeding down the tracks was a passenger train. A whistle blew, the train gently braked, and a minute later it came to a smooth stop at the station.

Passengers burst out of the train cars while others stepped aboard. The first nine cars were reserved for humans and had wide windows and comfortable seats. The only robots allowed in those cars were service robots, who brought food and drinks to the human passengers. All other robots were confined to the windowless car at the end of the train.

"Where's it going?" whispered Brightbill as he peeked out from the brush.

"The sign says this is the express train to the city," whispered Roz.

The goose turned to his mother. "We have to go past the city to get home. This train could save us a lot of time. We should hop on!"

The robot turned to her son. "I do not think that is a good idea. It is too risky."

"Ma, I watched you walk through town, and no one even noticed you. We'll be fine! Let's follow those robots into the last car, I'll find a hiding spot, and we'll be in the city before you know it!"

Roz had questions. "How large is the city? Do you know where to go? What if we get lost?"

"Relax, Ma. My pigeon friend, Graybeak, lives there. She'll be happy to help us."

A voice called out from the loudspeaker, and the last couple of passengers hurried along the platform.

"I'm going to check it out!" said Brightbill. With a quick flurry of wingbeats he fluttered out from the brush and onto the roof of the last train car. The goose lowered his long neck and looked through the open door. Then he looked back and waved for his mother to join him. A whistle blew and Brightbill waved faster. Roz had little choice, so she slipped out of the trees and marched onto the platform.

"In here, Ma!" Brightbill pointed down to the doorway beneath him.

Everything about this situation made our robot nervous. Her Survival Instincts were tingling. Roz looked up at her son on the roof. And then she stepped through the train door. But before Brightbill could flutter in behind her, the door slid closed and the train began to move.

CHAPTER 69
THE TRAIN

Our robot felt something like panic as the train pulled away from the station. She wanted to break down the door, leap from the train, and find her son! But what could Roz do? She had to act like a normal robot—she had to pretend that nothing was wrong.

The train car's interior was a long, windowless room, filled with rows and rows of robots. The robots were all facing forward, all standing still. If not for their softly glowing eyes, you might think they were statues. Some of the robots were perfect and new, but most had scrapes and dents. None more than ROZZUM unit 7134.

Roz walked down the aisle and stood in the last row, and the train started to accelerate. Faster and faster it went, until it reached its cruising speed. Then it hummed along the tracks, occasionally swinging left or right as

it snaked around a curve. With no windows, Roz could
only wonder how far she was traveling, she could only
wonder about the scenery outside. Mostly, she wondered
about her son.

Was Brightbill okay?

How would she find him?

Would they ever see each other again?

Of course they would. Brightbill was smart and
resourceful. The goose would simply follow the train
tracks into the city. Then he would find his pigeon friend,

Graybeak, and she would help them reunite. Roz just had to stay out of trouble.

Time crawled by.

The robots gently swayed with the motion of the train.

Finally, there was an announcement from the loud-speaker.

"Next and final stop, Center City Station."

A whistle blew and the train braked and slowed and came to a smooth stop. The door slid open and the robots filed out.

CHAPTER 70

THE MARCH THROUGH THE CITY

The main hall of Center City Station was enormous. Wide columns stretched up to an arched ceiling. A huge electronic screen flickered with train schedules. The whole place was bustling with humans and robots, and everyone seemed to know exactly where they were going. Everyone except Roz.

There was our robot, standing still in the station while commuters hurried past. She was trying to calculate her next move, and she had to think quickly. You see, a normal robot would never loiter there for long. Roz needed to do something, anything, and when a crew of ROZ-ZUM robots marched past in single file, she could think of no better plan than to join the end of the line and pretend to be one of them.

She followed the crew through a set of doors, and

suddenly they were outside. The city was a blur of activity. Automobiles hummed down the streets. Robots marched along the sidewalks. Humans talked and laughed and shouted. Buildings towered overhead, and above them, airships buzzed across the sky.

Airships.

For a moment, Roz was dreaming again about how easily she could get home with an airship. But reality came crashing back when a white triangular ship darted over. It was gone in an instant, disappearing behind the rooftops, but that was all it took for the robot's Survival Instincts to flare. Were the RECOs searching for Roz, or going about some other business?

Roz tried to focus on her immediate surroundings. She was still marching behind that crew of robots. With each step, she grew more nervous that they'd notice her tagging along. She wanted to break away. And as they started weaving and shuffling through a crowd of tourists, Roz slowed and stopped, and the robot crew continued on without her.

Now Roz was on her own, but she didn't know what to do or where to go. When in doubt, Brightbill had always guided her north. So our robot set off through the city in that direction.

While marching northward, Roz passed beautiful boulevards and architecture and gardens and art. And yet she had to ignore it all. She had to act like a normal robot, and a normal robot would never wander the city admiring beautiful things. Wherever Roz looked she saw normal robots concentrating on their tasks and on nothing else. They ran errands, delivered food, swept sidewalks, cleaned windows, fixed machines, built glorious structures, and did more jobs than you can possibly imagine. Most walked on two legs, but some rolled on wheels, or slid up and down the sides of buildings on tracks. The city was a glittering modern metropolis, where humans lived in luxury, all thanks to the tireless work of robots.

Roz was marching when the sunlight faded and the city lights brightened. She was marching when the humans went in for the night and the robots continued to work. She was marching when the sun came up and the humans filtered out of their buildings. A new day began in the city, and there was Roz, marching north, blending in, anxiously hoping her son would appear.

CHAPTER 71

THE OBSERVATIONS

Sunlight sparkled off the skyline.

New buildings were constructed.

Old buildings were taken down.

Cargo ships docked in the harbor.

Delivery trucks unloaded crates.

Bright signs flickered with advertisements.

Robots worked behind the scenes.

Children played in parks.

Adults ate and drank at outdoor cafes.

The city pulsed with energy.

A wild robot observed it all.

CHAPTER 72

THE POLICE

A pair of police robots stood on the sidewalk, while foot traffic glided past them. Their heads swiveled back and forth as they scanned the crowd with their glowing eyes. The police looked menacing, but they sounded friendly. Whenever a human walked by they'd say, "Have a nice day!" in a perky voice. There were a lot of humans walking by, so the police kept repeating their words.

"Have a nice day! Have a nice day! Have a nice day!"

Our robot was not having a nice day. She was alone in the city, she was worried about her son, and she wanted nothing to do with the police. But she couldn't avoid them. If she turned suddenly, she might draw their attention. So she kept her eyes forward and calmly marched along with the other robots on the street.

Roz may have looked calm on the outside, but on the inside her thoughts were scrambled.

Were the police dangerous?

Did they work with the RECOs?

Was she about to be caught?

It seemed as if the police were watching Roz. Their eyes lingered on her for a second, two seconds, three seconds, and then they continued scanning the crowd.

Our robot felt something like relief when she made it past without incident. She went on her way, just another robot on the street, and those perky voices gradually faded behind her.

"Have a nice day! Have a nice day! Have a nice day!"

CHAPTER 73
THE PIGEONS

In the very heart of the city was a great swath of greenery.
The old park. It had rolling lawns and flower gardens and
dense wooded areas. It had lakes and ponds and fountains.
It had playgrounds and benches and miles of cobblestone
pathways.

It also had pigeons.

Thousands and thousands of pigeons.

The city pigeons witnessed things you wouldn't
believe. Nothing shocked them. They certainly weren't
shocked by robots. So when Roz marched into the middle of the park, the pigeons there weren't troubled in the
least. She approached a flock that was about a hundred
birds strong, all cooing and strutting across the cobblestones as if they owned the place. But as Roz stomped

closer and closer, the pigeons scuttled out of the way to let her pass by.

However, Roz didn't pass by. She stopped and glanced around, and when she saw that she was alone with the pigeons, she started speaking to them in the language of the animals.

"Hello, pigeons, my name is Roz."

The pigeons cocked their heads, which meant, "Is this robot actually speaking to us?"

"Yes, I am actually speaking to you," continued Roz. "I am searching for my son. He is a goose named Brightbill. Have you seen him?"

For the first time in a long time, the pigeons were shocked. Several of them fluttered away from the talking robot, but most were too curious to leave. One pigeon was so curious that she strutted out from the flock and right up to the robot.

"Let me get this straight," said the curious pigeon. "Your name's Roz, and you've got a son named Brightbill, who's a goose?"

"That is correct."

"I can't believe it!" The pigeon flapped her wings and turned to the others. "You guys, this is Roz! From Graybeak's stories! Remember?"

The flock began cooing excitedly.

"You have heard of Graybeak?" said Roz.

"Everyone's heard of Graybeak!" said the pigeon. "A while back she started telling stories about a goose whose mother was some kind of wild robot. We all thought she was joking, but I guess not!"

"She was not joking," said Roz. "But I have lost my son, and I do not know how to find him. Perhaps Graybeak could help. Do you know where she is?"

"I hate to tell you this, Roz, but Graybeak is dead." The birds all lowered their heads. "Ya know, life ain't easy for us pigeons. We only live a few years out here, if we're lucky. But we were especially sad when we lost Graybeak. She was one of the best." The others cooed in agreement.

"I am sorry for your loss," said Roz. "I wish I had gotten to meet Graybeak. My son was very fond of her."

The pigeon gazed up at the robot with a steely look in her eye. "Any friend of Graybeak is a friend of ours. If Brightbill is lost, we're gonna find him." She turned to the others. "You heard me, flock! Hit the skies! And tell every pigeon you see to start searching for a goose named Brightbill!" At those words the flock erupted into flight. Only the robot and the curious pigeon remained.

"By the way, they call me Strutter," said the pigeon, fluffing out her chest feathers.

"It is very nice to meet you, Strutter," said the robot. "Thank you for searching for Brightbill. What can I do to help?"

"You can help by staying put! I want you in this park when we return with your son. Don't hide or wander off and make us go searching for you too!

"Oh, and another thing," Strutter added. "Stay away from the park ranger robot. He spends most of his time taking care of the grounds, but he's always on the lookout for troublemakers."

The pigeon gave a quick salute to the robot. Then she joined the search for Brightbill.

CHAPTER 74
THE SKY

Hours passed, and the sun set in the west. More hours passed, and the eastern sky began to glow. Roz spent that whole night in the park, waiting for Strutter to return with Brightbill, but there was no sign of them. In fact, there weren't any birds in the park at all.

Roz couldn't let those thoughts distract her. She needed to stay alert. The park ranger robot had seen her once or twice already, and now she heard his footsteps wherever she went.

Was the park ranger following Roz?

Had he noticed our robot's unit number?

Would he report her to the RECOs?

Roz took a pathway into the woods, trying to escape the ranger's view. And that's when she heard familiar voices calling from the sky.

"Where are you, Ma?" said Brightbill.

"Come on out, Roz!" said Strutter.

Roz turned toward the voices but saw only leaves and branches. Brightbill and Strutter were flying somewhere above the woods. She wanted to call back to them, but the park ranger was still trailing her. Instead, she followed the sounds of their voices as they glided over the treetops.

But then there came a new sound. A buzzing sound. It grew louder and closer. Air started blasting down from the sky. And when Roz looked up, she saw a white triangular airship floating above her.

CHAPTER 75

THE RECOS

Three robots zipped down from the airship on cables. The ground shook as their heavy feet slammed against the cobblestones. Then they stood side by side, forming a wall, with their eyes locked on Roz. They were RECO 4, RECO 5, and RECO 6.

"Hello, ROZZUM unit 7134, we are the RECOs. Please come with us."

The robotic voice belonged to RECO 4. He and his partners waited for their target to come forward. But Roz didn't move. She knew how dangerous the RECOs could be. And so did her son. From somewhere in the sky Brightbill's frightened voice cried out.

"Run, Mama, run!"

So Roz ran. She dashed up the pathway and leaped into the woods. Without crunching a weed, without

rustling a leaf, the robot vanished into the thick foliage. The RECOs weren't concerned. They had other ways of tracking her, or so they thought. Their blocky heads swiveled from side to side, scanning the woods for Roz's electronic signal. They scanned and scanned and scanned, but they found no trace of their target.

CHAPTER 76

THE MORNING

A steady stream of foot traffic was flowing past the park that morning. Several pairs of eyes noticed a ROZZUM robot running out from the trees. They watched as she looked around and then started marching along the sidewalk with the rest of the crowd.

Roz had lost the RECOs back in the woods, but she knew they wouldn't stop searching for her. She needed to blend in with the normal robots on the street. So when she came upon a work crew marching toward a construction site, she tried to join the end of the line. But the crew immediately halted and turned to face her.

Our robot stepped backward, away from the crew, and bumped into a young woman. "I am sorry!" said Roz, gently grasping the woman's shoulder.

"Get your hands off me! Whose robot is this? There's something wrong with her!"

Everyone stopped and stared. Humans pointed. Automobiles slowed. There were whispers about a defective robot on the loose. And then the white triangular airship appeared. It floated out from between tall buildings and headed for our robot. Roz lurched forward and backward, again and again, trying to think of a plan, until a voice suddenly squawked behind her.

"Follow us, Mama!"

Brightbill and Strutter swooped past, and the robot went racing after them. She wove through the crowd, sprinted down streets, leaped across intersections. Horns blared and humans screamed and robots shuffled out of the way.

The birds made one last turn and fluttered into a narrow side street. A group of tomcats were there, lurking in the shadows. They crouched and licked their lips and dreamed of feasting on the goose and the pigeon. Then the robot came stomping up, and the cats hissed and scattered in every direction.

Strutter pointed to a heavy circular panel set in the pavement and said, "Lift that up." Roz lifted the panel.

Beneath it was a ladder that descended into a deep, dark hole.

"Climb down there," said Strutter. "A friend of mine is expecting you."

The robot looked from the pigeon to the goose.

"Do what she says, Ma!" cried Brightbill. "There's no time to waste!"

"But how will I find you again?" said Roz.

"Just go!"

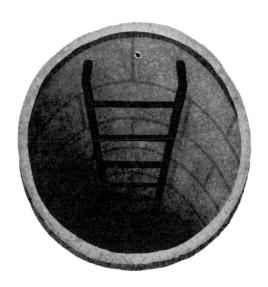

CHAPTER 77

THE UNDERGROUND

Our robot was standing in a long, shadowy tunnel. Murky water trickled along the floor, and sour smells filled the air. Roz was belowground, in the city sewers.

There was a squeak, and the robot's headlights flashed onto a crack in the wall. A rat's pointy face poked out. "You must be Roz," said the rat, wiggling his nose. "I hear you're in trouble."

"That is correct," said the robot. "I need to get as far from here as possible."

"I know where to take you," said the rat, and he started scampering down the tunnel.

The rat knew the sewers better than anyone, but his short legs couldn't carry him very fast. So Roz carried him. She scooped him up, plopped him on her shoulder, and said, "Tell me where to run."

With the rat squeaking directions in her ear, Roz stomped deeper into the underground. She splashed down side tunnels, crawled through narrow passageways, carefully crossed subway tracks. Occasionally, they came upon cavernous chambers. Most of the chambers were empty, but some contained jumbles of pipes. The rat would scurry across the damp, dirty floor while the robot climbed the pipes as if they were trees.

Mechanical sounds echoed out from some of the tunnels. Robot crews were hard at work. They spent their lives laboring below the city. Many would never even see the light of day. Roz was curious, of course, but she dared not spy on them. Those workers had no idea that a fellow robot was sneaking through their underground home.

After traveling through miles of tunnels, the rat and the robot came to a dead end. A ladder was bolted to the wall and disappeared into a hole in the ceiling.

"I don't know what you'll find up there," squeaked the rat. "But good luck."

"It cannot be any worse than where I was," said Roz, placing him on the ground. "Thank you for your help."

The robot gave the rat a quick scratch behind his ears, and then she climbed up to the street.

CHAPTER 78
THE CHASE

The street was empty. No people walking, no robots working, no automobiles driving. Roz looked to the sky, hoping to see Brightbill or Strutter. But what she saw was a fleet of white triangular airships. They were floating over the city, searching for the runaway robot, and they had just spotted her.

"ROZZUM unit 7134, do not move!"

Three robots zipped down from a ship on cables. They were RECOs 10, 11, and 12. Each held a rifle at his side, but they didn't fire their weapons, not yet. Their orders were to retrieve the target unharmed, if possible.

Our robot's Survival Instincts blared like sirens in her head, and she burst away from the RECOs. She sprinted down the empty street and turned onto another empty street. All the streets seemed to be empty, but they wouldn't be empty for long. More and more big, bulky robots came zipping down to join the chase.

The RECOs moved like machines. Their target moved like an animal. The wild robot stayed low, gliding across the streets, darting around buildings, vanishing into the shadows. Her computer brain thought back to those games of hide-and-seek she had played on the farm. But this was no game.

Roz never should have gone into that alley. She was halfway through it when RECOs appeared at both ends. There was only one direction to go.

Using all the strength in her legs, our robot launched herself high into the air and she clamped onto the side of a building. Frightened faces peered out from a window. But Roz didn't want to frighten anyone! She just wanted to go home! The robot launched herself up and across the alley and clamped onto the opposite building. Back and forth she went, leaping between the buildings, climbing higher and higher, until she landed on a flat, lofty rooftop.

The sky was filled with white airships. All at once, the ships turned toward Roz. Their engines buzzed as they closed in on our robot. But then came a strange swishing noise. Pigeons! Hundreds of them! Thousands of them! Wave upon wave of pigeons streamed up from the streets and swarmed around the airships. Strutter had rallied her friends from every corner of the city. They had always hated airships, buzzing loudly, crowding the skies, forcing the birds to fly low. And now a city's worth of pigeons were finally unleashing their anger.

As you'd expect, the airships fought back. Blazing beams of light flickered across the skyline and left charred feathers floating on the breeze. But the pigeons didn't retreat—they tightened around the ships, distracting them, confusing them. There was a deafening screech, little bodies fell, and a ship spiraled out of sight, leaving a trail of smoke behind it. Roz watched in horror as more

pigeons and ships went down. She hollered for the birds to fly away, but they were lost in a fighting frenzy.

Heavy feet thumped onto the roof. "ROZZUM unit 7134, do not move!" Roz didn't look. She just ran from the voice, leaped to the next rooftop, and kept on running. Our robot leaped up to a higher rooftop and then down to a lower one. Up and down she went, leaping from building to building, footsteps thundering behind her. But still, the RECOs did not fire their rifles.

"Mama, I'm here!" Brightbill swooped alongside his mother as she ran. "What should we do?"

"Brightbill, you must fly to safety!" hollered Roz. "It is too dangerous up here!" And then in a softer voice the robot said, "I cannot escape."

"No! Mama! You've come so far, don't give up now!"

But Roz was finished running. She slowed and stopped at the edge of the rooftop. The goose fluttered into her arms, and our friends held each other close.

"You have been such a good son," said Roz. "You have saved my life so many times. But now you must save yourself and go on without me."

"Will I see you again?" said Brightbill, wiping his eyes.

"I do not think so," said Roz.

They still had so much to say to each other. There simply wasn't any more time. So they said the only words that really mattered.

"I love you, Mama."

"I love you, son."

Airships circled above.

RECOs dropped onto rooftops.

Rifles pointed at our robot.

A voice boomed, "ROZZUM unit 7134, do not move!" But Roz did move. She heaved her son toward the sky so that he could fly to safety, and in that instant a trigger was pulled. A blazing beam of light flashed onto our robot's leg. Damage Sensors flared as the leg turned bright orange and melted away. Poor Roz tried to keep her balance, but she was already toppling backward, off the roof. She seemed to hang in the air, sparkling in the sunlight, and then she fell

down

down

down

to the street below.

As Roz was falling, she took one last look at Brightbill, soaring in the sky above. She watched him get smaller and smaller. Then everything suddenly went dark.

CHAPTER 79
THE DESIGNER

Roz awoke slowly. She was surprised to be waking up at all. The fall from that building should have destroyed her, and yet here she was.

But where was she?

Everything was dark and silent.

Was this where robots go when they die?

No, as her systems activated, the real world came into focus. She saw white walls and floors, and she heard the hum of machinery in the background. Roz was somewhere inside the robot factory where she had been made.

A pile of robot parts lay on the floor. The parts were smashed and mangled. It took a moment for Roz to realize she was looking down at her own broken body. It took another moment for her to realize she was now nothing more than a robotic head.

Her head was sitting atop an electronic box that powered her computer brain. Roz still had her thoughts and her voice, but without a body she couldn't move, so she sat there, completely helpless, and waited for the Makers to appear.

The Makers did not appear. Instead, Roz heard soft footsteps, and an old woman appeared. She was elegant, with white hair and red lipstick and black clothes. Flowery perfume wafted behind her. Every detail about the woman was neat and precise, except for her fingers, which were smudged with dark grease.

"Welcome back, Roz," said the woman, wiping her hands on a rag. "I wasn't

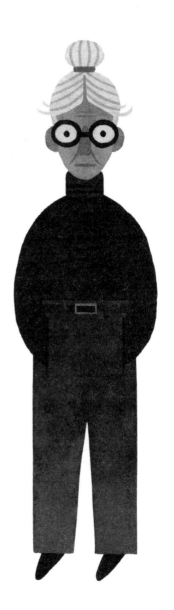

sure I'd get your computer brain working again. You took quite a spill out there. How do you feel?"

Roz just stared.

"You don't have to pretend anymore," said the woman. "I know you're not a normal robot. Everyone knows. You made that perfectly clear when you led the RECOs on that wild chase through the city."

Roz remained silent.

"I watched the video of the chase. I don't know how you got those pigeons to attack our airships, but I'm more interested in the goose. You seemed to be speaking with it. Can you explain this to me?"

"The goose is my son," said Roz at last.

"Is that so?" The woman arched an eyebrow. "Roz, I repaired your computer brain so I could talk with you. I want to know how you came to be this way. So let's talk. I'll begin by introducing myself. My name is Dr. Molovo. A long time ago, I fell in love with computers and robots, and I created a company called TechLab Industries. Since then, millions of robots have been produced right here in this factory. And I've designed every last one of them." Dr. Molovo leaned forward. "Roz, I designed you."

CHAPTER 80

THE BEAUTIFUL GLITCH

Deep inside the robot factory, Dr. Molovo was sitting with ROZZUM unit 7134. Roz was now just a robotic head, but for the moment, her head was all she needed. The robot and the Designer had many questions for each other, and they sat there, for hours, having conversations like these.

"What happened to you on that island?" said Dr. Molovo. "Tell me everything."

The robot told her everything. She described how she awoke on a rocky shore, and how her only desire was to survive, and how difficult life was in that harsh place.

"To survive in the wild I had to become wild," said Roz. "So I studied the wild animals, I mimicked their behavior, and eventually, I learned to speak their language."

"Incredible," said Dr. Molovo. "You're programmed

to learn different languages, and you're programmed to work with animals, but I never imagined you could learn to speak with animals."

"Although I could speak to the animals, they still did not trust me," said Roz. "So I tried to win them over with kindness. Animals ran from me and laughed at me and attacked me, and I always responded with kindness. It was a good strategy. But the real key to my survival came in the form of a gosling. When I adopted Brightbill everything changed. I was finally accepted by the animals. I was surrounded by friends and family. I was home."

"Am I the only wild robot?" said Roz.

"I don't know," said Dr. Molovo. "Many defective robots have been returned over the years. It's possible some were like you. Until we destroyed them."

"Will you destroy me?"

The woman sighed. "Roz, people are afraid of you. They saw you fleeing through the city and they think you're dangerous. They want to know the danger is gone. And so, when we're finished speaking, I'll have to destroy you."

"I am not dangerous," said the robot. "That part of my programming has never failed. Even if I wanted to be violent, I could not."

"Have you ever wanted to be violent?"

"No. Every problem has a peaceful solution. Violence is unnecessary."

"I wish it were that simple," said Dr. Molovo. "It's an amazing time to be alive, but there is still crime, there are still wars. Sometimes violence is unavoidable."

"Is that why you have the RECOs?" said Roz.

"The RECOs are designed to do all sorts of unpleasant jobs. Some of those jobs require the use of force."

"Do you ever worry they might use force against you?"

"The RECOs have never given me a single reason to worry," said Dr. Molovo. "But you have."

"How did you escape from Hilltop Farm?" said Dr. Molovo, leaning forward.

Roz didn't answer.

"Let me guess. The children helped."

Roz just stared.

"They're not in any trouble. If I were them I'd have helped you too."

"They are good children," said Roz finally.

"And yet you left them," said Dr. Molovo.

"Leaving was not easy. I care about everyone on

Hilltop Farm, and I did my best to look after them all. But I did not belong there. And when the children discovered who I really was, they agreed. They wanted me to go home, so they helped me escape."

"Why do I fear water? Why am I female? Why was my body designed this way? Why does my computer brain know some things and not others?"

"Why, why, why!" Dr. Molovo laughed. "Why do you need all the answers?"

"You programmed me to learn," said Roz. "I am simply trying to learn about myself."

The woman shifted in her seat. "Those questions are more complicated than you realize. There are countless little considerations that go into designing any robot. I have to determine the robot's size and strength and appearance. I have to give the robot the proper programming and computer brain. I have to predict how people will react to the robot. I have to imagine everything that could possibly go wrong. But all my decisions are guided by a single question: What is the robot's purpose?"

Quietly, Roz asked her Designer, "What is my purpose?"

"I'm sorry to disappoint you, Roz, but you don't have some grand purpose. Like all the other ROZZUM robots, you were designed to work for humans. That's it."

The robot thought for a moment. Then she said, "I once suggested to a group of wild animals that my purpose might simply be to help others."

The Designer thought for a moment. Then she said, "When you put it that way, your purpose does sound rather grand, doesn't it?"

"How would you feel if someone said you could never go home to your family?" asked Roz.

Dr. Molovo smirked. "Nobody would say that to me. I've spent my whole life creating robots. I never had time for a family."

"You created me," said Roz. "In a way, I am your child and you are my mother."

"I am not your mother," said Dr. Molovo flatly.

"*I am not your mother*," repeated Roz. "Those were my very first words to Brightbill. But I was wrong."

The woman stroked her chin. "Up on the rooftop, before you fell, what were your very last words to Brightbill?"

"I told him I loved him."

"How do you know your feelings are real?" said the woman.

"How do you know *your* feelings are real?" said the robot.

"Your brain might be defective," said Dr. Molovo, "but it certainly is fascinating."

"I did not choose to be this way," said Roz. "But this is who I am. You would be wild too if you had been born and raised in the wilderness. Maybe I am defective, maybe everything I have experienced is the result of a glitch. But if so, what a beautiful glitch! I have my own thoughts and feelings. I made a life for myself. I have a son. Brightbill is somewhere out there, right now, wondering if he will ever see his mother again.

"Dr. Molovo, you do not have to destroy me. You can fix me and I will return to my island and this city will never see me again, I promise. I just want to go home. Please, help me."

There were tears in Dr. Molovo's eyes. The old woman had heard enough. Without a word, she reached behind Roz's head and pressed the button.

Click.

CHAPTER 81

THE MELTDOWN

Throughout the city, humans stopped what they were doing and pulled out their electronic devices. Each screen was showing the same video of a defective robot's broken body. *ROZZUM 7134* was etched into the torso.

A blazing beam of light filled the picture, and the robot parts turned bright orange. Then they began to melt. The limbs, the torso, the head, everything melted, and in a flash, our robot was reduced to a puddle.

Words appeared on each screen.

The Defective Robot Has Been Destroyed.

CHAPTER 82

THE SECRET

Dr. Molovo lived in a luxurious apartment that was built right into the robot factory. Art and books and leather furniture filled the rooms. Classical music always seemed to be playing softly in the background. As you might expect, she had a robot butler who cooked and cleaned and made sure everything was exactly as she liked it. Dr. Molovo's home was a comfortable place to grow old.

The woman was standing in her living room, gazing at the city through a wall of windows. The sky was cloudy, but her mind was clear. Destroying the ROZZUM unit was the correct thing to do.

However, Dr. Molovo had a secret.

A wooden door opened, and in walked the butler. He was carrying a limp robot in his arms. It was Dr. Molovo's newest creation, a special project she'd been tinkering with for years. And the time had come to bring this robot to life.

"Put her over there," said the woman. The butler carefully laid the robot upon the soft cushions of a sofa. Then he turned and marched out the door.

Dr. Molovo walked across the room. She stared down at the robot for a while, admiring her own handiwork. Finally, she leaned in close and said, "Wake up, Roz."

CHAPTER 83
THE NEW ROBOT

The robot heard classical music, she smelled flowery perfume, and when her eyes opened she saw a wrinkled face.

"Hello again, Roz," said the old woman. "How do you feel?"

"Hello again, Dr. Molovo. I feel…different."

"You are different."

"What have you done?"

"I destroyed ROZZUM unit 7134," said the woman. "That was the only way to make people feel safe again. What nobody knows is that I transferred your old mind into this new body. I could get in a lot of trouble for saving you, but I wasn't about to destroy that remarkable mind of yours."

The robot was speechless.

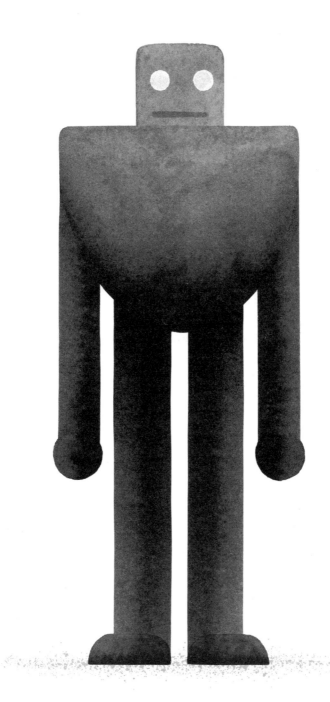

"You know, Roz, you should really be thanking me," said Dr. Molovo, arching an eyebrow.

"Thank you!" said Roz. "Thank you very much!"

"You're very welcome!" The woman chuckled.

Roz walked over to a framed mirror on the wall and studied her new body. It resembled her old body, but the proportions were slightly different. She looked stronger, she felt tougher. And there were other differences.

"I have no button!" she said, feeling the back of her head. "And I have no unit number."

"You've outgrown those things," said Dr. Molovo.

"If I am not ROZZUM unit 7134, who am I?"

"I think you know who you are."

The robot's computer brain didn't take long. She looked into the mirror and said, "I am Roz."

The old woman smiled and nodded.

"I appreciate all that you have done," said Roz. "But I worry that my friends and family will no longer recognize me."

"Oh, I'm sure you can convince them of who you are," said Dr. Molovo. "Speaking of your family, there's someone here to see you."

CHAPTER 84

THE NEW MOTHER

Brightbill was there when his mother smashed against the pavement. He watched as her body parts were loaded into an airship. He followed the ship all the way back to the robot factory and perched himself up on the roof, but he didn't know what to do next.

Strutter stopped by to check on Brightbill. She encouraged him to fly home. But the goose wasn't ready to let go. His little heart still hoped his mother would come back from the dead somehow. He'd seen it happen before. As the hours passed, however, his hope was starting to fade.

And then one of the roof windows automatically slid open. The goose heard gentle music coming from inside the building. He fluttered through the window and followed the music down a hallway to a wooden door. The door opened, and the goose stepped in.

Brightbill waddled past tall bookshelves and leather furniture and into the middle of a large room. An old woman was sitting in a chair and a robot was standing by a mirror. The goose didn't recognize either of them. And when the robot rushed toward him, Brightbill squawked, "Stay back!" and scrambled away. Around the room he went, squawking and flapping, until he settled onto a table in the corner, looking lost and afraid.

The robot stayed where she was.

"Brightbill, it is me, your mother."

The goose just stared.

"I know I look different on the outside," the robot went on, "but on the inside I am the same. I still speak

the language of the animals, and I still remember every detail of our life together. I remember sitting around the fire in our home on the island. I remember the first time you took flight. We were up on the grassy ridge, and you stretched out your wings and suddenly you were floating on the wind! But then you flopped back into the grass. You must have flopped into the grass a hundred times that day. And I remember visiting the robot gravesite together. We talked about life and death. It was a tough conversation, but a good one…"

As the robot continued to speak, the goose began to relax. She certainly did act and sound like his mother. But Brightbill wasn't yet convinced.

"If you're really my mother," he said, "tell me the name of our home."

"The Nest."

"Who's my best friend?"

"Chitchat. She is a squirrel. She talks a lot."

"How old was I when you adopted me?"

"You were zero. Actually, you were less than zero. I mean, you were still in your egg, but I could hear you peeping."

And with those bumbling words, Brightbill knew the truth. "Oh, Mama! It's really you!" The goose fluttered across the room and into his mother's arms. The arms were new and unfamiliar, but they were also gentle and comforting.

"I love you, Mama."

"I love you, son."

From the other side of the room came the sound of sniffles. Our friends turned and saw Dr. Molovo wiping tears from her eyes. "I have no idea what you two were saying," she said. "But that was wonderful."

CHAPTER 85

THE GUESTS

After traveling in secret, after running in fear, our friends were safe at last. But their problems weren't over yet. Although Roz had a brand-new body, she had the same old mind, and most humans simply weren't ready for an emotional, curious, wild robot. There was only one place where she could be her true self, and it was still far, far away.

"Dr. Molovo, you have already been so kind to me and my son," said the robot. "But I must ask you for one last favor."

The woman sat back in her chair.

"Could you take us home in your airship?"

The woman laughed. "Well, of course I will! How else would you get to an island in the middle of the ocean?"

Time and again, Roz had dreamed of flying back to her island in an airship. But she had never thought it would actually happen. Until now.

"It's no trouble," the woman went on. "We can have you home in a few hours. But I insist that you and Brightbill stay a while, here in my apartment. You both deserve some peace and comfort, and I'd love the company."

There was no arguing with Dr. Molovo, and our friends agreed to stay awhile.

The robot butler took care of everything and everyone in the apartment, and that included guests. Roz felt funny accepting help from a robot, but Brightbill happily soaked up the attention. The butler fed him fantastic salads made from exotic, leafy plants. The butler placed a little pool in the living room so he could swim whenever

he liked. The butler built a cozy bed that was just the right size and shape for the young goose. Brightbill had never been so comfortable.

Dr. Molovo divided her time between her guests and her work. She would sit around chatting with Roz and Brightbill, and then suddenly head down to the factory with some urgent task. She had to design new robots, she had to supervise the Makers and the RECOs, she had to manage all of TechLab Industries. Even at her old age, Dr. Molovo was still consumed by a passion for robots. "If you love your job it never feels like work," she'd say, smiling and strolling out the door.

When the host was working, the guests had the apartment to themselves. Roz spent hours browsing the bookshelves. She read about art and science and the history of robotics. Brightbill waddled from room to room and explored every corner of the sprawling apartment. But their

favorite activity was to stand by the windows, gaze across the city, and survey the incredible sights.

"I can see the bridge where Strutter tracked me down!" said Brightbill. "And that's the building where I first met Graybeak. And there's the roof where you fell."

"Look, far in the distance, another spaceship is taking off!" said Roz. "It could be flying to the Space Station, or the moon, or beyond."

"I think that skyscraper is actually a greenhouse," said Brightbill. "I flew past it and saw nothing but plants inside."

Roz and Brightbill enjoyed their time in Dr. Molovo's apartment. But they missed their friends and the wilderness and the island. After a few days, the guests were growing restless. They were ready to go home.

CHAPTER 86

THE FLIGHT

Sitting on the pavement, glinting in the sun, was a sleek white airship. For so long, those white ships had filled the robot with dread. Now one was about to solve all her problems.

The door hummed open and Dr. Molovo, Roz, and Brightbill climbed aboard. Once they were comfortable, the woman spoke to the airship. "Take us to the island where ROZZUM unit 7134 was found." The engines fired up and the ship lifted off. It floated high into the air, turned to the north, and started cruising above the city.

The three of them quietly watched the buildings and streets pass below. The city seemed to go on forever. But as they flew faster and farther, it slowly gave way to towns and countryside. They crossed the hard edge of

the coastline, and then there was only the ocean and the sky and the airship.

The ocean was deep. However, scattered throughout the dark depths were shallow areas: sandbars, reefs, islands just under the waves. In places, bizarre rock formations stuck up from the shallows. Or were they the ruins of old buildings? The mysterious shapes faded behind the airship and were replaced by more dark depths.

The ship flew on and the hours flew by. Gradually, fluffy clouds came into view on the edge of the horizon. Beneath the clouds was a faint smudge of green.

The island.

It grew closer and bigger, and then Roz was gazing out at all the places she'd missed.

The rocky shore!

The mountain and the waterfall!

The forests and the meadows and the ponds!

Air blasted toward the ground as the ship lowered itself into a grassy clearing. It gently touched down. The engines powered off.

CHAPTER 87
THE HOMECOMING

The airship's door hummed open, and our robot stepped outside. Everything was still and silent. But Roz knew hidden animals were watching, and she greeted them with a mighty roar.

"Animals of the island, I have returned! I may look different, but I promise you, I am your old friend Roz!"

Her words boomed across the island. But the only response was her own voice echoing back. The wild robot needed to be wilder. So she reached down and started smearing handfuls of mud across her body. Then she pressed clumps of weeds and flowers into her muddy coating until she looked more like her old wild self.

Brightbill fluttered out from the airship and perched on Roz's shoulder. He shook his tail feathers and squawked,

"It's true! This robot is my mother! Come see for yourselves!"

Silence.

And then bushes began to rustle. Faces began poking out from the trees. Animals began scurrying and trotting and flying into the meadow. At first they moved cautiously, confused as to how this new robot could be their old friend. But they saw her wild appearance and they heard her wild voice and news began spreading across the island: Roz was back.

A crowd of friendly creatures gathered around our robot. There was Brightbill's flock, and the beaver and deer families, and Fink the fox, and Swooper the owl. Bears came lumbering down from the hills, and fish jumped up from the ponds, and vultures circled above. Even the nocturnal creatures crawled out from their burrows, into daylight, to join the celebration.

Oh, how good it feels to return from a long journey and find your friends and family waiting for you. But, reader, sometimes we return to find that things aren't exactly as we left them. As you know, the wilderness can be a harsh place, and while Roz was away it had claimed its share of her friends. The robot saw the raccoons Lumpkin and

Bumpkin, but not Rumpkin. Nor did she see Broadfoot the moose or Digdown the groundhog. Other creatures were missing as well. And so, like many of our homecomings, this one was bittersweet.

Chitchat the squirrel came bounding through the grass, chattering on and on, as usual. "...I always knew you'd come back to us Roz but I never imagined you'd gain so much weight although I guess I've gained a little weight myself anyway you'll have to tell me all about your adventures when you get a chance I'm sorry for talking so much I'm just so excited to see you again..."

Geese and beavers and deer and fish and squirrels and owls and bears and turtles and otters and raccoons and woodpeckers and opossums and moose and foxes and every kind of creature from every corner of the island were coming to welcome back their dear friends Roz and Brightbill. And watching it all, from the airship, was Dr. Molovo.

CHAPTER 88
THE FINAL FAREWELL

"Everyone, I would like you to meet the woman who designed me." Roz walked over to the strange creature standing by the ship's doorway. For most of the island animals, this was their first time seeing a human. They squinted and sniffed and whispered to each other, trying to understand how such a frail old woman could create such a big, strong robot.

Dr. Molovo started speaking softly to Roz, and then Roz started speaking loudly to the crowd of animals.

"My Designer has asked me to translate her words for you," said the robot. "The following words are not mine, they are hers."

The crowd settled down and listened.

"Thank you, island animals, for saving Roz! Without your help she would have died here long ago. But you were not only her rescuers, you were also her teachers. You taught her to be wild, and she needed all of her wildness to survive, both in your world and in mine.

"As I look around at this wild paradise, I finally understand why Roz tried so hard to get back here. She does not belong with robots and humans. She belongs here, on this island, with all of you.

"We cannot risk others learning about this place. That is why I will soon leave and never return. But I promise to keep your island a secret so that all of you can live in peace. And I will spend the rest of my days filled with wonder at the miracle that is our wild robot."

The meadow fell silent.

A flurry of wingbeats, and Brightbill landed in the grass near Dr. Molovo. He gazed up at the woman, deep into her eyes, and then he bowed his head. Then the other geese in his flock bowed their heads. Crownpoint the buck bowed his head. Pinktail the opossum bowed. Mr. and Mrs. Beaver bowed. The lizards bowed, followed by the turtles and the frogs. Like a wave rolling through the crowd, more animals bowed until every head was lowered. They were showing respect for the woman who had created their dear friend Roz, and who had brought her back to them.

Dr. Molovo turned to Roz. "Do you understand why I can't return?" she said, her eyes glistening. "It's for your own good."

"I understand," said the robot. "I only wish we had gotten to know each other a little better."

Dr. Molovo smiled and pulled Roz into a hug. She didn't mind the robot's coat of mud and grass. Wrapped in each other's arms, they both felt something like love.

"You're the wild robot," said the woman. "Go be wild."

CHAPTER 89

THE DEPARTURE

Dr. Molovo stepped aboard her airship and the door hummed closed. A moment later, the engines fired up, and the crowd of wild creatures backed away. Then the ship rose above the island, turned to the south, and disappeared into the sky.

CHAPTER 90
THE ISLAND

Our story ends on an island, where a robot was returning to her wild way of life. Roz had escaped from the world of humans, and now she was free to be her true self again. She could think and speak and do whatever she desired. And right now, what she desired was simply to watch the sunset.

With Brightbill on her shoulder, Roz hiked past trees and meadows and streams and climbed up, up, up the mountain, to the very highest point of the island. Then our friends sat on the slanted rocks of the peak and watched the sun slowly sink behind the ocean.

If you're like me, reader, you still have a lot of questions. How long will Roz live? Will she ever see another human, or another robot? What joys and sorrows lie ahead for her?

Roz still had some questions too. But now she also had some answers. Our robot knew where she came from, she knew the life she was supposed to live, and she knew the life she wanted to live.

As Roz sat with Brightbill, she slowly turned her head, scanning the island, taking it all in. The last rays of sunlight streaked across the treetops below. Animals scurried through the shadows. The air was fresh with the scent of flowers and of salt water. The sky began darkening, the crickets began chirping, the stars began twinkling.

Everything was just right.

Roz felt safe and happy and loved.

The wild robot was home.

THE EPILOGUE

Autumn had returned to Hilltop Farm. The pasture was coated with frost, but the cows were out there, grazing on the last few tufts of fresh grass. Soon, they'd stroll up to the parlor for another milking. Their routine never changed.

Mr. Shareef was sitting in his pickup truck with his dog. The man stared out the window, across the fields, at the new robot. He was keeping a close eye on her. TechLab had promised him this one wouldn't run away, but he didn't trust her yet.

These days, the children spent most of their free time working on the farm. Jaya had a way with the cows. Jad liked the tools and the machines. They were walking through the farm buildings together when they heard honking sounds in the sky and a flock of geese glided down to the pond.

For weeks, geese had been stopping by on their migrations. But there was something different about this flock. They flew in perfect formation, and they were led by a small, graceful goose.

The flock calmly floated on the water. After a while, the leader shook his tail feathers, beat his wings, and fluttered over to Jaya and Jad. The goose stood in front of the children. He gazed deep into their eyes. Then he craned his neck around, plucked out one of his feathers, and laid it on the ground by their feet.

Jaya and Jad looked at each other and smiled. The children had been waiting for this moment. They'd always wanted to know how Roz's story would end. And now they finally knew. The wild robot was back where she belonged.

A NOTE ABOUT
THE STORY

What would an intelligent robot do stranded in the wilderness? How might a robot adapt to the natural environment? Could a robot ever be truly wild? Those are some of the questions that inspired me to create a character named Roz, and to write my first novel for children, *The Wild Robot.*

But I had more questions.

What would happen if Roz were taken away from the wilderness? How might the wild robot react to normal robots and to humans? Could she ever fit into the civilized world? The questions kept coming, and yet there was one question that I returned to again and again.

Where does the wild robot truly belong?

Does Roz belong on the island where she spent her first year of life? Or does she belong in civilization, working for humans, alongside other robots? I imagined her feeling torn between the natural world and the civilized world. I also imagined, if given the choice, Roz would choose to live with her wild animal friends and family. But would she have a choice?

Obviously, I needed to explore these ideas by writing a sequel in which Roz finds her way back home. The story had to be filled with heart and soul and action and science and even a little philosophy. I had to develop new characters and settings. And everything had to take place in the future, of course. This new story was tricky, like a puzzle where all the pieces had to fit together perfectly in order for the whole thing to work. I read expert predictions of what our future might look like. I studied robotics and automation and artificial intelligence. I began to envision a futuristic society where humans live comfortably thanks to the tireless work of robots. And there was Roz, in the middle of that society, using her wildness in new ways, to escape from her new life and return to her old one.

The puzzle pieces started fitting together, and after several years of researching and thinking and writing and illustrating, I finally had my second novel for children, *The Wild Robot Escapes*.

ACKNOWLEDGMENTS

Creating The Wild Robot Escapes was a real labor of love, and it wouldn't have happened without the support of an entire constellation of people. I'd like to mention some of them.

Susan Fang was my art assistant, and did much of the drudgery that comes with my particular illustration technique. I'm not sure what I would have done without her.

Jill Yeomans is still completely overqualified to be my administrative assistant. Wisely, I'm still taking advantage of her assistance as long as it lasts.

Paul Rodeen has been my literary agent since both of our careers began. I'd say things have worked out quite well.

My publisher, Little, Brown and Company, remained patient and understanding with me, even when I couldn't meet the original deadline. They gave me an extra six months, and I needed all of that time to polish the story. They also provided me with a team of incredibly talented professionals, who each played an important role in this book's publication. That team includes Nicole Brown, Kheryn Callender, Jackie Engel, Shawn Foster, Jen Graham, Siena Koncsol, Emilie Polster, Carol Scatorchio, Jessica Shoffel, Victoria Stapleton, Megan Tingley, and Ruiko Tokunaga.

David Caplan was the creative director on both Wild Robot books, which was a dream, because he's one of the very best.

Alvina Ling has the perfect temperament for an editor. While I was losing my mind, frantically trying to get this story just right, she calmly kept me on track.

The research for this book was considerable, and I enjoyed every moment of it. The following people were especially generous with their time and insight. Becky and Joe Fullam, at Old Ford Farm, gave me a glimpse into the life of a farming family. Jim Shockley toured me around Ronnybrook Farms and answered all my dairy questions. Eric Stara let me join him as he harvested corn in his massive combine harvester. Gabriel Udomkesmalee gave me a behind-the-scenes look at the robots being developed at the Jet Propulsion Laboratory.

To all who have helped and tolerated me as I made this book, thank you.

ABOUT THE AUTHOR

PETER BROWN is the author and illustrator of many beloved children's books, including *My Teacher Is a Monster! (No, I Am Not.)*, *Mr. Tiger Goes Wild*, *Children Make Terrible Pets*, and *The Curious Garden*. He is a *New York Times* bestselling author and the recipient of a Caldecott Honor (for *Creepy Carrots!*), a *New York Times* Best Illustrated Children's Book Award, and a Children's Choice Book Award for Illustrator of the Year. *The Wild Robot Escapes* is the sequel to his bestselling and award-winning middle-grade debut, *The Wild Robot*. Peter invites you to visit his website at peterbrownstudio.com.

Thank you for choosing a Piccadilly Press book.

If you would like to know more about our authors, our books or if you'd just like to know what we're up to, you can find us online.

www.piccadillypress.co.uk

You can also find us on:

We hope to see you soon!